CH00842421

BIR. GLAM. EDUC. AUTH.
1929
...TH COUNTY C. SCHOOL

Miscellany Two

Miscellany Two

Emyr Humphreys

———

POETRY WALES PRESS
1981

PUBLISHED IN 1981 BY POETRY WALES PRESS
56 PARCAU AVENUE, BRIDGEND, MID GLAMORGAN

ISBN 0 907476 05 8 Miscellany Two (Hardback)

ISBN 0 907476 06 6 Miscellany Two (Paper Back)

Copyright ©in this miscellanea Emyr Humphreys 1981.

*All rights reserved. No part of this publication may be reproduced,
stored in a retrieval system, or transmitted in any form or by any means,
electronic, mechanical, photocopying, recording or otherwise,
without the prior permission of the author.*

*The publisher acknowledges the financial assistance
of the Welsh Arts Council*

PRINTED IN 10 pt. BASKERVILLE
by
BRIDGEND PRINTING COMPANY LIMITED
TREMAINS ROAD, BRIDGEND, MID GLAMORGAN

Contents

Stories

Boys in a boat	9
A corner of a field	21
Down in the heel	35
The arrest	45

Poems

Interim verdict	61
A tree waiting	62
Partial recall	63
Two generations	64
Brân	67

Essays

Poetry, prison and propaganda	69
Arnold in wonderland	81
The loss of incantation	101
Television and us	111

'Down in the heel' was first published in the *New English Review;* 'A corner of a field' (a chapter omitted from *Outside the House of Baal)* in *Mabon* 1, spring 1969; 'The arrest' in *Madog* 1, spring 1978; the poem, 'The father', appeared in *Cyphers* 8; 'Poetry, prison and propaganda' in *Planet,* June 1978; 'Arnold in wonderland' in *The Powys Review,* summer 1978; 'The loss of incantation' in *Welsh Music,* winter 1973; 'Television and us: reflections on a troubled relationship' is based on lectures published in *Taliesin,* December 1974.

Boys in a boat

Norbert sprawled over the bottom of the boat, his long legs bending over the seat on which he could have been sitting neatly to observe the seamanship of the twins or at least the way his licensed tormentor had the tiller under his right arm. At fifteen Norbert had been stretched on a rack of growth to an abnormal height. His joints hung so loosely that they appeared to need tightening. With a hand behind his curly head, he smoked a woodbine defiantly and addressed a seagull floating between the blue sky and the top of the mast.

—In view of the fact, seagull, that you have been compared to a fist of sunlight, a fleck of foam flying, and a lily of the sea, and a love messenger, and a something or other incandescent flame, you may now bugger off.

He was delighted with the depth and resonance of his own voice. It was securely part of his being, although still not a year old. It more than made up for the loose gangling awkwardness of his limbs and his shambling gait. As he lay in the boat, the sound and the sophisticated knowledge to which it gave expression entitled him to some token of admiration from his companions.

—Shut up, Norbert Jones!

Only John Frederick at the tiller had the time or the inclination to listen to him. The twin brothers who owned the boat were obsessive sailors. Frank and Harry moved about the boat in their rope-soled shoes, tireless and surefooted, full of activity, determined to attain a perfection of order in their craft that would earn it a first prize from some invisible nautical judge. Norbert was in the way. They stepped over him and whether he spoke or sang, paid him little attention. John Frederick was allowed in charge of the tiller as a special concession. He had pleaded to be allowed to steer with such insistence that Frank thought it would be churlish to refuse so importunate a plea from the spoilt favourite of one of the most prominent families in the town. His brother Harry was less willing. He only gave way because of the possibility that it would be something Frank wanted. That was the way the twins functioned, like a tandem where the rider in front always senses the direction his partner wishes to take.

Norbert broke out in song. It was not unpleasant. A juvenile bass-baritone still uncertain of its power. He closed his eyes to

11

attempt a higher note and the squeezed sound quickly spent itself in such a vast expanse of summer sea. The seagull was un-disturbed in threading the contours of its own territory. Norbert lifted his head briefly as though to check that the view which surrounded them was still there. Mountains for a radius of more than fifty miles and the lower slopes with identifiable villages, forests, castles and farms. They were well away from the land and yet not in the open sea: between them and the sands of the estuary there was a white line that shimmered in the sunlight. Frank looked back at the centre of the crescent where the breakers were bigger and wilder in their successive rows. He was experiencing in retrospect the thrill of crossing the bar. Harry could sense this. Sailing gave their easy world-less understanding extended practice.

—'A sailor boy am I, my home is by the sea . . .'

Norbert made his bid for their attention and approval.

—Well that's a lie to begin with!

John Frederick had an explosive manner of speaking which he had copied from his father who was a colonel in the Volun-teers.

—You are a peasant, Norby and not even a decent poet! Whoever heard of a poet called Norbert Jones?

—You just wait!

Norbert tried to think of some clever reply and failed to find one. With a lordly gesture he tossed his cigarette stump into the sea. For a while all was silent except for the creaking of the boat and the slap of indolent waves against the side. A squad of young puffins waddled towards the point where the cigarette stump had first touched the water. Norbert propped himself up to watch them over the gunwale. Their curiosity seemed greater and more purposeful than his.

—Boys, Norbert said in his deepest voice. Fellows. You know, this is what it will be like in heaven. 'Hot sun and puffins. Hot tea and muffins.'

—Just listen to the idiot.

John Frederick uttered a ritual expression of contempt. Harry and Frank were busying themselves producing what they called their picnic tea. Their movements were as swift and as sure as ever. There were buns already buttered, sea biscuits in

12

which they took a special pride, oatmeal-water and elderberry wine.

—To think we only brought him along as ballast. And to provide a bit of entertainment . . .

John Frederick pointed at Norbert.

—Just look at him. A cross between a piece of seaweed and a dogfish.

He slapped his thigh, he was so pleased with his sally. Frank handed Norbert a tin mug of oatmeal.

—Nectar, Norbert said. Food for the gods.

Harry and Frank sat down to enjoy their meal. Frank was in charge of the wooden spoon. He dipped it into the porridge meal at the bottom of the half-gallon milk can. He sucked it appreciatively and looked over the side to study the seabed.

—Looking for German subs, Frank? John Frederick said.

Frank took the question seriously. The twins were not given to badinage.

—No chance, he said. A sub would never get in and out of these waters alive.

—Oh, I don't know.

John Frederick was most reluctant to give way to Frank's nautical expertise. He was a leader of opinion in his generation. And there was always the question of his personal prestige. It was something that had to be worked at, constantly reinforced. In this boat and on this afternoon, if left unattended it could dwindle to a pin-point and even disappear into the deep. John Frederick automatically made his first thrust in the direction of Norbert.

—Jones, Norbert! How old was the Black Prince at the Battle of Crecy?

—Eighty-nine, Norbert said.

—I'm not joking you fool. This is a serious question. With a serious bearing. Do you know, Frank?

To ask Frank was also to ask Harry. Both shook their heads.

—No idea, Frank said.

—Sixteen.

John Frederick pushed the fact out explosively. It was a statement of great significance. He spoke as an authority on military matters. His tone was deliberately clipped and precise.

—He led the attack at the age of sixteen.

13

—Get away.

Frank was suitably impressed and so was Harry. They were on the threshold of their sixteenth birthday: born within a few minutes of each other, either side of midnight.

—Now it's a curious fact . . .

John Frederick adjusted the tiller under his arm. He pulled a face and squinted at the sun to conceal the fact that his information had been picked up recently in a magazine and was not something he had been privy to for many years.

—It's a curious fact that in the British Army soldiers under twenty cannot be sent to serve on foreign soil.

—Quite right too, Norbert said.

—Oh shut up you flabby jellyfish.

John Frederick was annoyed that such serious issues should be taken lightly by inferior creatures of childlike mentality.

—Army Regulations, he said.

He was determined to assert himself.

—There is one way of getting round it of course.

He paused to make sure that the other boys were listening.

—Join up as a bugler.

Norbert put his fists to his lips and blew an imaginary fanfare.

—You blithering idiot. I can tell you this much. There was a bugler in the Rifle Corps who was killed at the Battle of Aisne. He got a D.C.M.

Frank and Harry were impressed again. They glanced at each other long enough to decide not to ask what the initials stood for.

—There were twenty bullet holes in his bugle, John Frederick said.

His voice was solemn enough until he saw that Norbert was smiling as he blinked up at the seagull.

—What are you grinning at, you blithering bard?

—It sounds a bit funny, Norbert said. That's all.

—I dare say you'd look funny too. With twenty bullet holes in your bugle.

John Frederick's large mouth opened suddenly to let out a hoot of laughter. Quite unexpectedly, he knew he had invented a memorable joke. The others joined in. The phrase was repeated. Even Harry said it.

Their laughter fed on itself until it reached the verge of hysteria. Norbert was holding his stomach to contain the pain. Frank was the first to sober up. Harry was quick to follow suit. They busied themselves putting away the remains of the picnic tea and preparing to set a course southward. Frank had a yachting cap stuck at a jaunty angle over his untidy hair. Harry wore a knitted cap with a red tassle. John Frederick made jokes about how the headwear helped to tell the difference between them.

They set to work trimming the sails. John Frederick sat up, ready for once to take orders. Norbert was sent to crouch in the bow. The sheets tugged and the leech quivered and more sea-gulls appeared above the mast, screeching away as if the prospect of human movement and the speed of a boat across the deserted waters gave them a fresh aim in life. Norbert peeped over the side at a school of porpoise following their wake. He tried to whistle to them as though the leaps they made out of the water were a response to this call. Frank and Harry tacked to windward, silent and efficient and as ever quietly pleased with the chance to demonstrate their dexterity. Norbert was so intent on communicating with the porpoise he leaned too far out. The unexpectedly cold air made him shiver so much he could no longer control his whistle. Frank who noticed everything to do with the well-being of the boat and its passengers, made a brief gesture and Harry produced a thick fisherman's jersey from a locker and made Norbert put it on. John Frederick called out some disparaging remark but it was lost in the wind. Norbert stood up unsteadily, intimating that he would be the first to catch a glimpse of the sunken city. He began to use his deep voice again.

—Listen to this, chaps. 'Let the waves dance where the barley grew and wide cold water cover the trees . . .'

—You'll see something in a minute!

Frank shouted close to Norbert's ear. John Frederick was deprived of the tiller. Harry took charge. The whole expedition now was in the expert hands of the twins. Norbert recited some more.

—'O fields of life where children played
    And church bells rang in the sun . . .'

—Rot!

15

John Frederick shouted out.

—It's all rot. Tommy rot. Rubbish.

—Hold on now.

Frank was ready to argue. He looked disturbed, even shocked by John Frederick's heretical blasphemy.

—It's history isn't it? he said. You can't call history tommy rot.

—Legend, John Frederick said. Myth and legend. What else? In other words, Tommy rot.

—Hold on then. Watch this then. I'll prove it. Here and now. See over there?

Frank leaned out to point to the south-west. What looked like a bank of stones or a long ruined wall was already creating its own sea of turbulence in the reasonably calm sea. As they sailed closer they saw rows of sea birds perched on the damp pinnacles, quite unperturbed by the angry churning of the breakers.

—Now, Frank said. Now then John Frederick. See over there? There is a gap in the Sarn where the sluice gates were. And we are going to go right through it!

Harry seemed to know what he was saying, although he could not possibly have heard the words. Frank made one gesture and their course was set. The boat was taking a head-on course for the causeway called *Y Sarn*. It lay ahead of them like a snaky sleeping monster stretching painfully westwards, endlessly resentful at having its lumps and scaly excrescences washed by the urgent antiseptic sea. Norbert let out a wail and closed his eyes. Somewhere there was a gap, if the twins said so: but he couldn't see it. He was resigning his fate to their seamanship. He sank down to his knees, clutching the gunwale, letting his long body rock and sway with the boat.

When he opened his eyes he saw shags and puffins to the leeward, still clinging to the pinnacles and perches and absorbed in their own statuesque stillness. They were through the gap and sailing easily once more in calm water. The risk was over.

—What's happening, men?

Norbert sounded so deflated and bewildered that both John Frederick and Frank burst out laughing. John Frederick appropriated some portion of the triumph to himself by slapping Frank heartily on the back.

—Now it's the return ride, Frank said.

The boat sailed in a smooth circle and this time Norbert determined to keep his eyes open. Frank was pointing to glimpses of what he claimed were great slabs of worked stone, fallen masonry covered with seaweed and barnacles. He even claimed to see traces of mortared walls. He became so excited that he neglected his duties until Harry gave a warning shout from the tiller. The boat gave an unexpected lurch. Norbert held on and was suddenly sick over the side. He sank exhausted to the bottom of the boat and never made the detailed inspection Frank wanted as they passed through the gap.

When they reached calmer waters the twins showed equal concern for Norbert's condition. The sails were lowered. John Frederick was allowed to repossess the tiller. Harry offered Norbert a spoonful of wet oatmeal to suck. He assured the groaning bass-baritone that this was a sovereign remedy. Frank produced a large green bottle from the locker and ordered Norbert to take a swig. The liquid was so fiery it made him cough.

—Fire-water, bottled in hell, he said.

He cheered up when he saw the others laugh. His response was included in the repertoire of memorable remarks. John Frederick insisted the whisky bottle should go the rounds.

—Well I know one thing for certain now, he said, wiping his mouth with the back of his hand.

—Of course you do, man, Frank said. You've been through Seithenyn's sluice gates. What did I tell you?

—Rubbish.

John Frederick was confident and categorical.

—Old wives' tales, he said. Absolute rubbish.

Frank and Harry were troubled. Norbert frowned and held on to his stomach.

—All we saw, gentlemen, was natural phenomena. All that stuff is nothing more than natural deposit.

—But it's a straight line, Frank said. A straight line for twelve miles or more.

—Wave action, John Frederick said. Glacial deposits and so on. As a matter of fact we've done it in geography. It's all there for you to see if you know the scientific rules.

Frank nursed the large green bottle. The beliefs of the sea-

17

faring folk he and Harry belonged to were being challenged and so was their pride. Those hidden lands under the sea were solid parts of their collective imagination. Why had they been reduced in their own boat to disconcerted silence? Frank looked at the cork of the bottle as if he considered taking a second deep swig.

—I tell you one thing.

Norbert had recovered sufficiently to speak.

—They were more interesting anyway. And more beautiful.

—Rot.

John Frederick was becoming more and more relentless.

—Science, he said. That's what's interesting. The future belongs to science. You know what Kitchener says.

The other three looked submissive. They were ready to be instructed.

—When this war is won, the British Empire will be the most powerful Empire the world has ever seen. So you know what that means?

He had become so emphatic that they listened to him with awe.

—The British Empire and Modern Knowledge will rule the world!

Norbert was moved to make his small protest.

—I don't know about that man, he said.

John Frederick turned on him furiously.

—Don't know what, frogspawn?

—That Kitchener, Norbert said. Doesn't want us to have our Welsh Army, does he?

John Frederick shook his head pityingly.

—It just shows you, he said.

He appealed to each of the twins in turn as men of common sense and sound judgement.

—What happens when you let blithering bards loose in matters they know nothing about. We've got the whole world at our feet and this idiot goes blathering on about his Welsh army. What are they going to wear, Norbert? Nightshirts and bloomers?

Once again he slapped his thigh and let out a hoot of laughter. The others were slow to join in. He was forced to repeat the phrase twice and poke first Harry and then Frank in the ribs before he gained the response that he coveted. Norbert waved his hand weakly to show that he too was willing. He would have laughed as heartily as any of them if only he could find the strength.

—Kitchener for ever!

He held on to the side of the boat.

—Rule Britannia, bois bach down there. Rule Britannia!

The effort was too much for him. With a deep retching sound he vomited again into the sliding sea, dangling over the gunwale like an abandoned sacrifice.

Three lined footnote on the imagined fact:

Second Lieutenant John Frederick Williams, killed in action, March 1918.

Frank and Harry Roberts, lost at sea, North Atlantic, November 1917.

Norbert Llewelyn Jones, died T.B. sanatorium, Talgarth, April 1923.

A corner of the field

The old tractor made so much noise, there was no point in talking. J.T. balanced his gladstone bag on the seat which was wrapped in an old sack. The driver, a melancholy faced man, explained he could not sit down himself because he suffered from piles. His bent knees served as shock-absorbers against the violent vibrations of the machine. J.T. clutched his hat with the hand that also held the umbrella and nodded sympathetically. Where the hedges were trimmed down, J.T. cautiously lifted himself to peer into the fields on the left side of the road as if he expected to see someone he knew. It was a hot day and he held his face gladly to the slight breeze caused by the tractor's progress.

The narrow road took them to the gates of Plas M—; there was a glimpse of an unkept drive disappearing between the dark trees. The tractor driver pointed to a gate to the left of the whitewashed lodge.

—Down there you go! That's the way to Allt Goch!

He shouted above the engine and J.T. showed his gratitude for the lift by nodding vigorously, tapping the man on his back, praising his Pembrokeshire Welsh, and getting himself and his belongings off the tractor as quickly as he could so as not to waste the man's time. For a moment the tractor driver looked at him suspiciously and then he smiled.

At the gate J.T. turned to wave. The driver waved back and steered his tractor through the gates, so that the noise of his engine was muffled abruptly by the trees. The track to Allt Goch appeared to pass through the gates of a series of fields, each gate to be opened and shut. J.T. closed the first gate and breathed deeply and listened to the warm sounds of the early afternoon. He touched the long foxgloves that grew out of the hedgerow. The ruts of the cart track were baked hard. Wearing his hat and dark mackintosh and carrying his bag and his umbrella he moved into the field in order to walk more comfortably. The field had been over grazed and it was covered with crusted cowpats and clumps of well-grown thistles.

He passed a muddy pond and an oak tree under which sheep were resting among their droppings on the cool earth. Then came a hay field that had been cut and carried. He put his case down in order to close the rickety gate. He took off his mackintosh and jacket and folded them to carry them over his arm. His face had already begun to glisten with sweat. In the next field he leaned against the hedgerow and seemed to consider taking a rest. He folded his arms and looked critically at the rows of swedes that stretched down the field. The leaves were perforated with the nibbles of insects and butterflies. As he walked on he looked down at his boots. By now they were covered with a film of dust. He changed his bag from one hand to the other as he walked. It was not large but there were books in it that made it heavy. Also the pockets of his mackintosh bulged with small parcels.

Alongside the next gate there was a tall stile. J.T. studied it carefully. He was able to clamber up without putting down any of his load. The summit of the stile was higher than the top of the gate and he balanced himself carefully on the narrow stone. The air was cooler and sweeter and there was a clearer view of the way ahead. After the width of two fields the land fell away and there was just a glimpse of the slate roofs of the farm among the trees. Beyond that, the woods on the opposite side of the valley merged in a blue haze. The view was so pleasing it made him smile.

He was also able to see over the wild hazel hedge on his left. A square five acre field had been closed off with a mixed crop of oats and barley. The crop was maturing too early because of the dry weather. It was when he turned back to look at the way he had come, that he noticed two human figures lying in the corner of the five acre cornfield. They lay in the long grass of the headland that had not been ploughed. A soldier and a woman, totally unaware that he was looking at them. The soldier's tunic was a pillow under the woman's head. The woman was naked from the waist down and the soldier's sunburnt arm stretched carelessly across her white thighs as if he were asleep. J.T. looked back at the roof tops of the farm. He peered up at the sky where an invisible skylark was singing. He looked again at the couple in the corner of the field. He was close enough to see that although the soldier was asleep with his face in the grass, the woman's eyes were open. Her white belly and her black pubic hair that were meant to be hidden, had become the centre of the whole landscape. She had not seen him. Instinctively he bent his head as if he himself had urgent need to hide. The soldier was stirring and might at any moment sit up and see him. At

24

the foot of the stile his mack fell to the ground and he dragged it along for some yards before stopping to pick it up.

Trees became more frequent as he came nearer the farm and kept it entirely in the shade, with a cool rustle of air in the leaves. For the last three hundred yards they grew on either side of the stony lane. His foot dislodged a stone and it tumbled forward down the lane that now sloped more steeply and J.T. had to bend his knees to keep his balance. A dog barked and he could hear it pulling at its chain. The back door of the farm house was in sight. The approach now was roughly paved with flag stones.

The back door was open. Still grasping his case, with his jacket, mackintosh and umbrella over his arm. J.T. called out in a cheerful voice. It was quite clear the house was empty and yet every door and window was open. He walked through to the front door and saw the excited sheepdog that rattled its tether in a corner of the yard sheltered from the sun. A layer of flaked dung covered the sloping yard and the doors of all of the out-houses were open. It was a prosperous farm that had been allowed to decay. At the side of the house there was a neglected orchard. The branches of the apple trees were covered in moss and lichen. Beyond the orchard there was a stony field that appeared to be over-grown with sorrel. In a corner of the orchard that had been cleared a pet lamb was grazing. Outside the barn there was a load of corrugated zinc sheeting and sea-soned timber. A restoration seemed in hand.

J.T. put down his coats and his case on the low wall that protected the narrow garden at the front of the house. He looked back as if considering whether or not to go inside the house again. He seemed deeply interested in everything he saw. He moved out into the middle of the yard. The dog stopped barking and watched him anxiously. He was drawn to a gate at the bottom of the yard. There was a view of the long narrow valley immediately beneath the farm. He leaned on the gate and saw the way in which the woodland on either bank of the little river was gaining ground on the neglected water meadows. The hedges between the meadows were overgrown and the irregular fringe of the woods could be seen spreading into the fields, a darker green, except where the breeze caught the light leaves of the sapling alders. In the furthest distance it was possible to see four or five men working, clearing the shrub and the woodland, and opening drains and ditches. Sometimes the sunlight seemed to flash on the blades of their mattocks. He shaded his eyes with his hands, steadying his elbows on the top bar of the gate.

—Can I help you?

A woman's voice called. He turned and saw her standing in the open doorway of the farmhouse. He walked back to the house with apologetic haste. The woman wore a skirt and blouse of the same silky material. It was the woman he had seen in the field. She ran her hands which were red from housework through her hair, which had been dyed jet black. Her face was older than her body. It was not a young girl he had seen in the field. On the bridge of her nose there was a weal which showed that she usually wore spectacles. The pupils of her eyes were so distended they made her blue eyes appear black and added to the air of anxiety that underlay her cultivated manner. She was an Englishwoman in her middle thirties.

—You must forgive me.

She offered her hand tentatively.

—I've lost my spectacles. I just can't find them anywhere. It's such a nuisance.

—I'm Vernon's father, J.T. said.

—Of course you are. You look just like him. Or vice-versa I should say. My name is Dorothy Colinson. We haven't met, but I think you may have met my husband. . . .

Her polite smile faded slowly. For a while he had been staring at her, speechless, and now as he turned his eyes away, he was blushing.

—It's very pleasant here, he said.

He pointed at the pet lamb in the orchard as a piece of evidence in support of his statement.

—Oh but the mess is terrible. Usually I have help but for the last three weeks I've had to manage by myself. Of course these days one mustn't grumble. Anyway, listen to me talking about myself. You must come in. We've got a big surprise for you. Someone you know very well.

J.T. followed Mrs. Colinson into the house. It took a few seconds for his eyes to accustom themselves to the gloom. In the kitchen, in a low armchair near the open hearth that stretched across furthest corner of the room, he saw his eldest son, Ronnie.

He was smoking and as he got up he exhaled the smoke from his cigarette, moving his head sideways to avoid bumping against the low beam. He pushed down a box of matches in the pocket of his battle dress tunic. He seemed self-possessed and at the same time his politeness was awkward.

—What are you doing here?

—I'm on leave, Ronnie said. They're carrying on the war without me for thirty six hours.

—Why didn't you come home?

—I'll leave you two together and get on with my work, Mrs. Colinson said. You'll have a lot to say to each other.

Across the passage she began to move pots and pans in the dairy as if to demonstrate that she wasn't listening.

—By the time I arrived it would be time to start back, Ronnie said.

—You ought to write oftener. Your mother gets so worried.

—I'm sorry, Ronnie said. I'm a rotten correspondent. There's always more I don't want to say than what I want to say.

—What do you mean?

—It was a joke.

—A joke?

Ronnie shrugged his shoulders and spread out his hands. J.T. moved his head to study the gesture closely as if it would give some clue to his son's character. They stared at each other.

—I think you're losing weight, Ronnie said. How are things in the chapel. Any more resignations?

—Your mother isn't at all well.

—She never is, is she?

—What do you mean?

Ronnie threw his cigarette away and stretched himself lazily.

—Nothing would do except a nice little middle-class church, in a nice little North Wales Watering-place.

—I don't like to hear you talk like that about your mother.

—I lost my Rugby and she gained her rheumatism. Or whatever it is she's got.

—She isn't at all well, J.T. said again.

27

He sat down suddenly. Mrs. Colinson was marching in and out of the dairy. Buckets clanked noisily as she set them up on the wall beneath the trees. She hurried about like someone making up for lost time. There were hens in fold-units in the field beyond the trees. She hurried over the low stile to feed them. J.T. could see her through the small kitchen window.

—Who is she?

He spoke so quietly Ronnie could barely hear him.

—Dolly? Dolly Colinson. You met her husband in Eights Week. Don't you remember?

—Where is he now?

—God knows. Ronnie said. They've separated. As you can see she's a woman full of ideas. I think he's in Intelligence. She's down here looking after a bunch of back-to-the-land conchies. Including our Vernon of course. I must say he thrives on it. Have you seen him?

—How could I?

—Brown as a berry and as strong as an ox. Doesn't smoke. Doesn't drink. Takes after you.

J.T. turned his head as he heard Mrs. Colinson climb over the stile. The stone paving between the wall and the house was dappled with the trembling shadows of the leafy tree. On the window shelf there was an old wireless set and a carbide lamp. Ronnie leaned across the table to switch the wireless on. There was nothing to be heard except oscillations and crackling. He switched off again.

—The news is terrible, J.T. said.

—Best news possible, Ronnie said. He had to break out to the East. If they can hold on for the next few months, the Russians will crush him.

—I'm thinking of the men women and children who will be slaughtered, J.T. said. That's what I'm thinking about. The cities in ruins. The countryside destroyed.

—From now on, we've got a real chance of winning. Best news for years.

—Nobody wins a war, J.T. said. Nobody.

He spoke vehemently.

—Don't let's start, Ronnie said. Not now.

—I can't stop bearing witness to what I believe is right because it isn't fashionable any more.

28

—Not now, dad. Please.

—I've seen war, my boy. I know what war is. This time it will be so much worse. Wales won't survive this war you know. What are you smiling at? I'd rather not live in a world where Welsh wasn't spoken. What are you smiling at?

—You are so muddled . . .

—Wales doesn't matter of course.

—What's Welsh got to do with it? What's Welsh got to do with war?

—That's all it means to you?

—We are dealing with a war. And if it comes to that, what's pacifism got to do with Nationalism, for God's sake?

—Everything, J.T. said. Everything.

—This is how you've always been, dad. Logic can't get any-where near you. If it had you would have been a socialist M.P. With you its all emotion and exhortation. Don't you know the Age of Exhortation is over? It's time to do things now. Look. You always talk about power as if it were something dirty. It's an instrument. Something to be used. I can remember saying all this to you when you stopped me going to Spain. It's still just as true. It isn't that I'm any cleverer than you or anything like that. There are certain facts you refuse to see because you wish they didn't exist. Anyway now is the time to fight. There is nothing else we can do. The issue is so simple. On any level. It's him or us. And he is evil. You admit that he's evil?

—No man is entirely evil, J.T. said.

—And worse than that, he's probably mad.

—It's ordinary Germans you'll be killing, not him.

—If he's mad and they all follow him, they're all tinged with madness. If they came here, people like you would be the first to be strung up. Luckily for you they'll never get here. Because people like me are going to stop them. And while we're on the subject I'll tell you something else. When it's all over, I'm not coming back. I don't want to live in an open-air museum. I want to go where ideas are made and where the future is shaped. Wales suffocates me.

—Then what are you doing here?

The question burst out so unexpectedly. J.T. poked the table angrily with his stiffened index finger. They heard Mrs.

Colinson taking her feet out of her clogs at the back door. They listened to her running through the passage and up the stairs in her bare feet.

—I suppose you expect me to believe you've come to see Vernon!

—Don't let's quarrel, dad. Please.

—You won't see the wickedness of war, J.T. said. The wickedness and the horror.

—I'm not afraid of dying. That's all. Not like poor old Vernon.

—He's no more afraid than you are, J.T. said.

—There you are you see. You can't see anything right in front of your nose. He's scared stiff. That's what all the talk boils down to.

—You're talking about your own brother.

—I know I am. I think the world of him and as far as I'm concerned he can go on talking about the holy soil of Wales as long as he likes. All I'm trying to point out to you is there is no more defenceless creature in the world than a chapel-bred Welsh poet. He has two skins less than anybody else.

—All you do, J.T. said, is to harden your heart to the suffering of others. That's all you do. Your own mother is ill and you won't come home to see her.

—There you are! Always the same! I can do nothing right. Not a thing. I am totally corrupt.

—Oxford, J.T. said.

—Yes, thank God. You weren't all that keen on my going there. Mam's bit of middle-class snobbery was a big help there.

J.T. had no answer.

—You know, dad, I don't think you've ever really forgiven me since I said Bayley Lewis was a homosexual. Something a boy of sixteen shouldn't think let alone say. Certain things should never be talked about.

Ronnie's mood changed suddenly. He laughed and slapped his father's shoulder.

—Oh dear, oh dear. We've had some rows in our time, haven't we? What's the news from the chapel front? How's that little squirt Dr. Emrys?

J.T. jumped up from his chair. He opened his mouth and

30

then closed it. He turned on his heel to leave the kitchen. The passage was darker than it had been earlier because Mrs. Colinson had shut the front door. He groped his way forward. When his eyes got used to the gloom, he saw that she had also hung his dark mackintosh and jacket on the row of hooks on the passage wall. His gladstone bag was on the stone floor immediately beneath them. J.T. reached for his jacket and put it on. As he did so he saw the inside of the front parlour. The door and the window were wide open but even on this summer day, the room smelt damp. There was a table in the centre of the room and on the floor stacks of books waiting to be put in the empty bookshelves on either side of the fireplace.

J.T. set his gladstone bag on the table and opened it. He pulled out a bundle of new Welsh books. There was also a piece of home-made slab-cake in a tin and a new shirt. In the passage he held up his mackintosh as he tried to pull out the packages that were wedged tightly into the pockets. Mrs. Colinson appeared on the stairs. She was wearing a shirt now and a pair of breeches.

—Let me help you, she said.

—I've brought some things for Vernon, J.T. said. Can I leave them on the table in there?

—Yes of course, Mrs. Colinson said.

Ronnie appeared in the passage. He put his hand on the banisters.

—A cup of tea would be nice, he said.

—Um.

Mrs. Colinson nodded girlishly and smiled. She pushed her fingers through her hair as if she were acutely aware of her appearance.

—I wish I knew where my specs were, she said. I can't get used to being without them.

She bent down and peered at Ronnie with exaggerated short sight.

—Where are you? she said.

—Oh Grandmama, what big eyes you've got!

—Kindly never refer to a lady's age, Mrs. Colinson said. I'm nobody's grandmother, thank you.

They were ignoring J.T. He took down his umbrella from

31

the hook, picked up his bag and put his coat over his arm.
Ronnie looked at him and grinned. He spoke to his father
playfully in Welsh.

—You look as if you're off to a preaching engagement, he
said.

—J.T. did not smile. He spoke in English.

—I'd better be going.

—Going?

—Would you tell Vernon his mother isn't too well.

He spoke to Mrs. Colinson and she nodded. She tried to steal
a glance at Ronnie but J.T. was looking at her intently so that
she was obliged to pay him her full attention.

—If he could ask for some leave, he said. I'd like him to come
up and see her.

—Look, dad. This is downright stupid. You can't leave without seeing him!

—He knows where we live.

Ronnie slapped his hand against the banister and raised his
voice.

—I'm stationed less than fifty miles from this place, he said. I
told you. It would take me all my leave just to get home and get
back.

—I'm not blaming you. You're old enough to . . .

—Blame! What's it got to do with blame? Everything's a
moral issue with you. It's nothing to do with right and wrong.

—We would like to see you both whenever you can manage
to get home, J.T. said.

—Don't start making a noise as if you were forgiving me.
I've done nothing wrong and I don't want to be forgiven thank
you very much. If you want to go off in a huff, you go off in a
huff.

Ronnie stepped aside and made a gesture of showing that the
way was clear for J.T. to go.

—A cup of tea, Mrs. Colinson said.

She was confused.

—There is so much to do in this place. . . . I've taken on too
much really. . . .

—Good afternoon, J.T. said.

—Mr. Miles. . . .

Ronnie held her by her arm.

—Let him go, he said.

J.T. halted in the back doorway. Ronnie walked towards him. J.T. swallowed and closed his eyes tightly for the fraction of a second. He appeared to want to speak again. He turned to look at Ronnie. The longer they waited the more difficult it became for either to say anything. At last J.T. turned and walked briskly towards the leafy lane.

Down in the heel

A cloud of white dust followed my Ford 30-cwt. down the road to San Donici. We passed a huge lumbering farm cart drawn by a little thin horse. I caught a glimpse of the sleeping carter the reins slack in his hard brown hands, and I thought of the dust he would unconsciously swallow through that open mouth.

'Rain,' said Signor Pesante, gazing morosely at the drooping leaves of the short vines. 'Everything is burning. Dio mio. Another bad year.'

We saw three women transplanting tobacco—six brown legs, three black skirts. It was a finely tilled patch of red soil on the roadside. An olive grove cast an uneven shadow on the edge of the field. The dusty cactus in the ditch stood stiff and undaunted by the heat.

Regarding the women Signor Pesante said: 'Very hard work tobacco transplanting.' I thought I detected a note of relief in his voice that he was seated alongside me in the truck, and not involved in the tobacco operation. Or perhaps he was congratulating himself, the son of a poor farmer, on his cosy dusty office in the Prefettura at Brindisi. I saw him close his eyes and raise his eyebrows. But that might have meant anything.

Signor Pesante had been specially assigned by the Prefect himself to assist me in my Refugee Work. After three exasperating weeks I began to appreciate the art of Signor Pesante. He was not as I had first thought, lazy, inefficient, corrupt, cowardly, stupid, although there were times when he seemed all these and more. Signor Pesante was an artist. He played the complicated antiquated enormous wind and paper instrument of Italian bureaucracy with the sure hand of a master craftsman.

'Do you mind,' he asked as we bumped into the outskirts of the village, 'stopping at the house of my wife's mother for just five minutes. Perhaps you would like a glass of wine. They are poor people, peasants, but they have good wine.'

We drew up before a white-washed house on the edge of the village. A bare-footed boy sat on the door step, as though in training for a long career of squatting in the sun. He screwed up his face in the sunlight, greeting us. Signor Pesante pulled his ear as he limped into the house.

'My sister-in-law's son,' he said.

Inside the family sat as though they had been waiting for us, in the front room, with the best bed and the photographs and sacred pictures on the walls. The father-in-law, a sunburnt grizzled peasant leaned on the table with his cap in hand and stared at me with rather an inane interest. The three (as I thought) unmarried daughters still in their teens, wearing very short skirts and dirty white blouses, clustered in the darkest corner and stared. The prematurely aged mother shuffled about in an old pair of her husband's boots and brought out a ceremonial tray of wine.

Signor Pesante carried on a brisk conversation in dialect with his relatives, exchanging family news and telling me in his odd English most things I was too polite to ask in Italian. He had long since understood that curiosity was my dominant vice.

'That little bitch is the most youngest,' he said, noticing where my glance had stayed. 'Poor little bitch. She has been destroyed.'

'She is only thirteen, poor little bitch. The man was twenty-one, a labourer of this village, and after he refused to marry her. And now he is dead.'

'When did this happen?' I asked.

'Last week. They found the bastard in a ditch last Thursday morning, knifed.'

'What do the police do?'

'I tell you this law is older than any other here. He destroyed her life and he must be destroyed. Here comes the man who did it. This, I think, the police know.'

A dull-looking peasant of about thirty years had entered silently and shaken hands with me. His hands seemed curiously cold and soft for a labourer. Otherwise he was not remarkable. He sat down behind the table in a posture that seemed a mime of his father's.

'And this bitch,' said Signor Pesante, 'wants to get married next month, to a good young man. She is sixteen. Her mother thinks it's better to get her married.'

He swallowed his second glass of wine. It was thick and black, stronger than I had ever tasted before. I could not follow a long animated discussion in dialect between my friend and his father-in-law, except to understand it was about a certain sum of money at the Banco di Napoli at Brindisi.

When we were back in the truck he said to me, 'They are

strange these peasants. My father-in-law thinks I am Mussolini's right hand because I have a post at the Prefettura.'

Mussolini: a tired worn old man trying to deceive himself that he wasn't doomed and saying last week at Brescia to the assembled faithful, 'Our securest peace lies in the shadow of our bayonets!' And last week Livorno had fallen.

'You understand Mussolini came and went without leaving much impression on my father-in-law.' Signor Pesante was laughing so engagingly, I believed it was a good joke too.

When we arrived at the Municipio we were both in a good mood. It was a fourteenth century stronghold built of local brown stone that was soft and worn and seemed to drain the massive building of any pretence of strength. In the courtyard we saw a dry fountain on which two porous-looking cherubs posed for flight. The building also contained the municipal prison. The warden sat outside the door, twiddling an enormous key, taking his duties very literally I thought.

'How's business?' Pesante greeted the warden as we passed.

'*Cosi, cosi,*' was the reply with an equalising motion of the out-stretched hand. The warden was in a greasy suit of civilian clothes and trilby hat. He wore a Partito d'Azione badge in his button-hole.

Upstairs we were met by the Communal Secretary, a very thin aristocratic-looking old gentleman wearing a panama hat. He led us to his office which to my mind seemed more like an archdeacon's study with all its leather-bound books and obscure oil-painting. Only after several minutes' polite conversation did I realise that his nerves were on edge.

'And when,' said Signor Pesante in his best manner, 'shall we have the pleasure of seeing his Worship the Mayor.'

'I must apologise,' said the Secretary, 'the Sindaco knew you were coming and was waiting to meet you when he was urgently called to the Police Station in the Piazza Cavour.'

'Trouble,' said Signor Pesante, a sympathetic note in his voice.

'I'm afraid so. Trouble.'

We observed a decent silence while the full flavour and meaning of the word possessed us all.

'When,' I ventured to ask, 'do you think he will get back?'

The Secretary regarded me in silence, making allowance no

doubt for my foreign origins, then shrugging his shoulders delicately he said,

'Who knows? Perhaps this evening.'

I did not want to make the journey to San Donici again merely because the Sindaco was engaged for an unspecified length of time at the Police Station.

'May we,' I suggested, 'go over to the Police Station in my vehicle and have our talk with the Sindaco there?'

'Very well,' the Secretary said slowly, and then with greater enthusiasm as though having viewed the idea from a new and profitable angle, he repeated, 'Very well: shall we go gentlemen. I shall accompany you. An excellent idea.'

As we approached the Piazza Cavour I began to understand the Communal Secretary's enthusiasm for my idea. The square was thick with people, a solid dark-clad throng of males. Solitary females caught unawares edging along the pavement were whisked off home by their indignant male relatives. The Ford nudged through the hostile, silent crowd at three miles an hour and I kept my thumb well down on the klaxon. As we drew up alongside the Police Station the heavy door was flung open and the Chief of Police with a very worried look on his face came out to greet us. He ordered two carabinieri to sit in the truck outside as we went in. They complied, rather unwillingly, I thought, with his order.

On the threshold the Chief of Police halted us and holding up his head said,

'Smell?'

And indeed there was a reek in the air, rather like petrol fumes and a smell of burning.

'What is it?'

'Two bodies were burnt in the Piazza about an hour ago, soaked in benzine.'

'Good God.'

We winced. The smell became overwhelmingly convincing.

The Sindaco sat in the Chief of Police's office biting his finger nails and listening to the Vice-Sindaco, a young foxy-looking man with the Communist badge in his button-hole. The Vice-Sindaco's calmness and smooth voice was conspicuous among so much agitation and suspense.

'I'm deeply sorry about it,' he was saying. 'I knew them both as children, Ubaldo and Ugo, but they should have known, times have changed. Besides, they ought to have understood that your being a member of the Sassoni family didn't mean the Sassoni family were still having everything their own way in San Donici. And then again, there's no doubt about it, they did say that they were uncompromising Fascists, and they did go about boasting that they would bring back the black shirts to San Donici . . .'

'Boys . . .' said the Sindaco, a burly white-haired man with sagging lower lip, wearing a light brown overcoat in spite of the heat.

'Barbarism . . .' said the Communal Secretary quietly in a tone of voice that made you feel that some day he would shout it from the house tops.

'I know . . . I know,' said the Vice-Sindaco gently, also one felt, with his eye on the future, 'but what can we do . . . the people . . .'

'The Communists . . .' said the Communal Secretary softly. There was, I felt, something snake-like in the thin frail looking old man. He had not taken off his panama hat.

'What happened?' I ventured to ask.

The Chief of Police burst out with the story. A bull-like man he told a story forcefully.

'Early this morning while the town was still sleeping a band of Communists broke into the house of Annamaria Aquapendente, a widow of the Sassoni family, and took her two sons, Ubaldo and Ugo, who returned last week from Tripoli. You might say the poor boys were out of touch with things. They were good boys, too, I'll say that for them, and never did anyone any harm, except that they were always rather extremely patriotic. They took the boys into the best room in the house, and shot them there, just as Annamaria Aquapendente was coming downstairs with a candle in her hand.'

He paused dramatically. The Sindaco got up and gazed through the window at the crowd in the Piazza. The Vice-Sindaco studied his finger nails.

'Bad eh? But they did worst. They dragged the bodies through the streets and, armed as they were, putting a devilish fear into every decent man and woman. And there in the Piazza they poured benzine over the bodies and set them on fire.'

41

I was tactful enough not to ask what the Police had done about it. I thought of Shelley entering Naples in 1819 and seeing a man being chased and knifed from where he sat in his coach.

'I shall not eat any dinner today,' the Chief of Police said sadly.

I glanced at Signor Pesante. He shook his head and shrugged his shoulders philosophically.

'The Refugees . . .' I suggested hopefully.

'Tomorrow,' the Sindaco said heavily.

'Besides,' said the Chief of Police, 'no one is safe if things like this are allowed to continue. Perhaps the Central Government could send down special police, or some soldiers even . . .'

'Humph.' The Sindaco evidently didn't give much for that idea.

'Don't worry,' said the Vice-Sindaco, and then shut his mouth again as though uncertain what to say.

At this point we all began to listen to the strains of a brass-band coming down towards the Piazza. It was playing an operatic funeral march. Everyone went out into the porch to watch the procession. The crowd in the Piazza made way for a boy in cassock and surplice with a white hood over his head, bearing on high a large brass cross. He was followed by two burly widows in black bearing aloft between them a gaudy blue and gold banner bearing a portrait of a virgin martyr. Then came two rows of children, with a young priest in the middle. When the band passed they began chanting.

'Viva Ghesu! Viva Ghesu!'

And the band in shabby uniform passed through the square in silence carrying ten large instruments.

The Chief of Police gripped my arm.

'There,' he said. 'Look there. Those two. They shot Ugo and Ubaldo.'

I looked among the expressionless faces of the bandsmen. It was useless. I couldn't guess which two the Chief was referring to.

Behind the band came four men carrying on their shoulders an image of the Virgin, in a blue cloak, with a wax doll's face and yellow flaxen curls. My companions uncovered their heads. Even the Communal Secretary took off his panama hat.

Out of the square the band struck up its solemn march again.

'Murder at seven. Festa at eleven,' said the Chief of Police bitterly as he pulled on his cap.

The Sindaco was claiming my attention.

'My dear young Sir,' he said, 'would you be so kind as to take me home in your motor-car? I'm feeling rather unwell, I must confess.'

'Certainly,' I replied, returning his bow.

'I'm so glad,' said the Chief of Police, smiling. 'I should not like to think of our honoured mayor walking the back streets on a day like this. In fact, if you will be so kind as to allow it, I shall accompany you myself. I live quite near the Sindaco. Not that I shall eat any lunch today,' he added.

The arrest

A short stocky man stood in the middle of a room lined with books. He was in his shirt sleeves. His clenched fists inside his trouser pockets pressed down hard so that the tough elastic in his braces was fully stretched. He shut his eyes and breathed deeply. When his tight lips expanded with the conscious effort of subduing his excitement, he looked pleased with himself. He opened his eyes. They were a piercing innocent blue. A beam of the morning sunlight caught the framed photograph of his college football team hanging above the door. He saw himself picked out plainly in the back row, his arms folded high across his chest a tight smile on his face, his head crowned with golden hair cut short at the back and sides and brushed back in close even waves. It was a head of hair to be proud of. A blackbird in one of the cherry trees at the bottom of the garden burst into a prolonged cadenza. His hand opened and passed softly over the trim white waves that remained to him, still cut close in the old style.

His wife appeared in the study doorway. Her grey head was held to one side. She dry-washed her long white hands and smiled at him winningly.

—I don't think they are coming today, Gwilym.

Her voice was quiet, a little tremulous with anxiety and respect.

—Cat and mouse.

His thumbs planed up and down inside his braces.

—It's obvious what they are up to. Cat and mouse. Trying to break my will. Trying to make me give in.

His wife lowered her head. Her concern seemed tinged with guilt.

—Let him stew a bit longer. You can hear them say it.

The room reverberated with his resonant nasal baritone. He was a minister who enjoyed the art of preaching. His wife's attitude of troubled and reverential concern urged him on.

—The magistrates were very polite. Very gracious. The narrow iron hand in the thick velvet glove. A month to pay. That month expired, Olwen, ten days ago. And still they have not been to get me . . . That's the way things are done in this little country of ours. It's all persuasion, moderation, compromise. As I said yesterday, an entire population is guided, herded like a vast flock by the sheepdogs of the communication media into the neat rectangular pens of public obedience. And we still don't realise that those pens are process machines and that we have all become units of mass government analogous to units of mass production: uniformed wrapped and packaged products of the state machine.

She closed her eyes before taking a step into the room. Her hands spread out in a gesture of pleading.

—Gwilym, she said. You've made your stand. The congregation understands and admires you. That's something a minister can be proud of. Why not pay now and have done with it!

He lifted a warning finger.

—I have forbidden any member of my congregation to pay my fine! I have made a legal statement to the effect that all our property, such as it is, including our little Morris Minor, is in your name, "Mrs. Olwen Dora Ellis". They can come when they like to arrest me.

She moved to the window and looked forlornly at their narrow strip of garden and the circular rockery they had built together. The aubretia was already in flower. The north wall of the chapel was faced with slates that looked less austere in the vibrant sunlight. The minister ran his finger lightly along a row of volumes on a shelf.

—The role of the church in the modern world et cetera et cetera, he said. How readily we take the word for the deed. It's deep in our psyche. What we need is more preachers in prison.

—Yes, but why you, Gwilym?

The question was intended as a humble appeal: but she could not prevent it sounding sulky. He waved it aside.

—Yes but where are the young ones? You are a man of fifty six, Gwilym. You have certain physical ailments sometimes . . .

—Piles, he said.

He spoke as one at all times determined to be frank.

—Otherwise I'm extremely fit.

—It worries me. I can't bear to think of you going to prison for a month.

—Twenty eight days.

—It really worries me. I don't think I can stand it.

They both stood still as though they were listening to the un-interrupted song of the blackbird in the cherry tree. He wanted

48

to comfort her but her distress embarrassed him too much.

—We've been over this before, he said. Somebody has to take a lead. Our language is being driven out of the homes of our people and our religion is being swept away with it. We *must* have an all-Welsh television channel. That's all there is to it. That's what our campaign is all about. When words fail, actions must follow. Stand firm, Olwen.

At last he moved closer to her and put his arm over her shoulders.

—Now what about a cup of coffee?

ii

It was while they sat in the kitchen drinking it, the police arrived. Mrs. Ellis glimpsed a blue helmet moving above the lace curtain.

—They've come, she said. Oh my God . . . they're here.

She stared so wildly at her husband, she could have been urging him to run away and hide. He sat at the table, pale and trembling a little. He spoke in spite of himself.

—Didn't think they would come today, he said.

The peremptory knock on the back door agitated Mrs. Ellis so much she pressed both her hands on her grey hair and then against her cheeks.

—I've got fifteen pounds in the lustre jug, she said. Do you think they'll take them, Gwilym, if I offer them?

The colour began to return to his cheeks.

—They don't really want you to go. The prisons are too full anyway. I read that in the paper only a week ago. They're too full you see. I meant to cut it out to show you. They won't have room for you, when it comes to it . . .

The minister breathed very deeply and rose to his feet.

—It's not a place for you anyway. Not a man like you Gwilym. This is your proper place where you're looked after properly, so that you can do the work you have been called to do. A son of the Manse living in the Manse. There isn't a man in the Presbytery who works half as hard as you do . . .

—Olwen! Pull yourself together! Be worthy.

A second series of knocks sent him rushing to the back door.

He threw it open and greeted the two policemen with exaggerated geniality.

—Gentlemen! Please come in! I've been expecting you and yet I must confess I'm not absolutely ready to travel, as you can see. Won't you come in?

He led them into the parlour. The room was conspicuously clear but crowded with heavy old-fashioned furniture. It smelt faintly of camphor. In a glass-fronted cabinet there were ceramic objects Mrs. Ellis had collected. Two matching Rembrandt reproductions hung on either side of the black marble mantlepiece. The minister invited the policeman to sit down. The senior policeman removed his helmet. A dull groove encircled his thick black hair. Sitting in a low armchair he nursed both the charge-sheet attached to a clip-board and his helmet on his knees. His companion stood at ease in the doorway until he realised that Mrs. Ellis was behind him. She recoiled nervously when he turned and pressed himself against the door so that she could pass into the room. He was a young policeman with plump cheeks and wet suckling lips. When she saw how young he was she looked a little reassured. The older policeman twisted in his chair to speak to her. His voice was loud with undue effort to be normal and polite.

—I don't expect you remember me?

She moved forward to inspect his face more closely. His false teeth flashed under his black moustache and drew attention to his pock-marked cheeks and small, restless eyes. The minister's wife shook her head a little hopelessly.

—I am Gwennie's husband. Gwennie Penycefn. You remember Gwennie.

—Gwennie . . .

Mrs. Ellis repeated the name with affectionate recognition. She looked at her husband hopefully. He was still frowning with the effort of identification.

—You taught her to recite when she was small.

Mrs. Ellis nodded eagerly.

—And Mr. Ellis here confirmed her. I don't mind telling you she burst into tears after breakfast. When I told her where I was going and the job I had to do. "Not Mr. Ellis" she said. "He baptised me and he confirmed me". Poor Gwennie. She was **very upset**.

The minister nodded solemnly. He stood in front of the empty fireplace, squaring his shoulders, his hands clasped tightly together behind his back. The armchair creaked as the policeman lowered his voice and leaned forward.

—What about paying, Mr. Ellis? You've made your stand. And we respect you for it. It's our language too isn't it, after all. I don't want to see a man of your calibre going to prison. Honestly I don't.

—Oh dear . . .

In spite of her effort at self-control, Mrs. Ellis had begun to sigh and tremble. The policeman turned his attention to her, gruff but confident in his own benevolence.

—Persuade him, Mrs. Ellis bach. You should see the other one I've got waiting in the station. And goodness knows what else the van will have to collect. The refuse of society, Mrs. Ellis. Isn't that so, Pierce?

He invited a confirming nod from his young colleague.

—Scum, Pierce said in his light tenor voice. That one tried to kill himself last night, if you please.

—Oh no . . .

Mrs. Ellis put her hands over her mouth.

—Younger than me too. Now he needs a stretch. Do him good.

—Officer.

The minister was making an effort to sound still and formal.

—This man you say tried to kill himself. What was his trouble?

—Drugs.

The older policeman answered the question.

—Stealing. Breaking and entering. Driving without a licence. Drugs.

The policeman spoke the last word as if its very sound had polluted his lips. His colleague had managed to tighten his wet lips to demonstrate total abomination. He made a strange sound in his throat like the growl of an angry watchdog.

—Will you give me a moment to . . . dress . . . and so on?

The policeman sighed.

—You don't need anything, my dear Mr. Ellis. You go in wet and naked like the day you were born.

Mrs. Ellis moved into the crowded room. Even in her distress

51

she navigated her way between the furniture without ever touching their edges. Her arms floated upwards like a weak swimmer giving in to the tide.

—I'll pack a few things, she said. In your little week-end case.

Her eyes were filling with tears and it was clear that she had not taken in the policeman's last words.

—Wear your round collar, Gwilym, she said.

She spoke in a pleading whisper and made a discreet gesture towards her own throat.

—There's still respect for the cloth, isn't there?

—I go like any other man who has broken the English law, he said. Get me my coat, Olwen. That's all I shall need.

The younger policeman looked suddenly annoyed.

—Look, he said. Why cause all this fuss for nothing? It's only a bit of a telly licence. Why don't you pay the fine here and now like any sensible chap and have done with it?

The minister looked at him.

—You have your duty, he said. I have mine.

iii

The rear door of the van opened suddenly. The minister had a brief glimpse of men out in a yard smoking and enjoying the May sunshine: they were plain-clothes men and policemen in uniform. They paid little attention to the van, even when a bulky youth in frayed jeans was lifted bodily and pushed into it. He collapsed on the cold metal floor near the minister's feet. His large head was a mass of uncombed curls. When his face appeared his lips were stretched in a mooncalf smile. He was handcuffed and there were no laces in his dirty white pumps. His wrists were heavily bandaged in blood-stained crepe. His nose was running and he lifted both hands to try and wipe it. A plain-clothes detective bent over him, still breathing hard.

—Now look, Smyrna, he said. You promise to behave yourself and I'll take these off. Otherwise you'll be chained to the pole see? With a ring through your nose like a bull.

Smyrna was nodding and smiling foolishly.

—You've got a real minister to look after you now. So you behave yourself and I'll bring you a fag before we leave.

His boots stamped noisily on the metal. The slamming of the rear doors reverberated in the dim interior of the police van. Smyrna, still sitting on the floor raised his arms to stare at his wrists. The minister nodded at him and moved to make room for him on the narrow bench. Smyrna's tongue hung out as he searched the pockets of his jeans for a cigarette. He found a flattened stump, rolled it between his dirty fingers and stuck it between his lips.

—Got a match?

The minister felt about in his pockets before he shook his head. He looked apologetic. The young man sucked the wet stump. He lifted his bandaged wrists so that the minister could observe them.

—You know what he said?

—Who?

—That sergeant. That detective sergeant. "Didn't make a good job of it, did you?"

The minister leaned forward to scrutinise the lateral scratches ascending both the young man's strong arms.

—That's sympathy for you. I was upset. It's a terrible thing to happen to anybody. Eighteen months in prison. And that was all the sympathy I got.

The minister gathered up the ends of his clerical grey macintosh and leaned forward as far as he could to show intense sympathy.

—How did you do it?

Smyrna's lips stretched in a proud smile, the cigarette stump still in the corner of his mouth.

—Smashed my arms through the glass. Thick it was. Frosted. Too thick really.

He mimed the act of scratching his arms with pieces of broken glass. Then he pulled a face to indicate his pain. The minister was distressed.

—Is it hurting now? he said.

—Aye. A bit.

Smyrna's head sank on to his chest.

The van lurched abruptly out of the yard. Through the small window the minister caught a glimpse of familiar landmarks warmed by the brilliant sunshine: boarding houses, a deserted slate quay, a wooded corner of the island across the sandy straits. Smyrna was on his knees communicating with the two policemen who rode in front. A plain clothes man the minister had not seen before, lit a cigarette in his own mouth and then passed it between the bars to the young prisoner. Smyrna settled at last on the bench, enjoying the luxury of the smoke, staring most of the time at the bandages on his wrists, lifting first one and then the other for a closer inspection.

The minister asked him questions. He wanted details of his background. As the van travelled faster the interior grew colder and more draughty. Smyrna's eyes shifted about as he tried to work out the ulterior motive behind Mr. Ellis' probing solicitude. He pulled his tattered combat jacket closer about his body and sniffed continuously to stop his nose running. His answer became monosyllabic and he began to mutter and complain about the cold and the noise. His eyes closed. He sagged in his seat and his large body shook passively with the vibrations of the uncomfortable vehicle.

The van turned into the rear of a large police headquarters. It reversed noisily up a narrow concrete passage to get as close as possible to a basement block of cells. Smyrna jerked himself up nervously and called out.

—Where are we then?

The minister tried to give a reassuring smile.

—I've no idea, he said.

The van stood still, the engine running. There were shouts outside and the jovial sounds of policemen greeting one another. Smyrna's mouth opened and his eyeballs oscillated nervously in their sockets as he listened.

When the doors at last opened a smartly dressed young man jumped in. He wore large tinted spectacles and his straight hair was streaked and tinted. He wore his bright handcuffs as if they were a decoration. He sat opposite the other two, giving them a brief nod and a smile of regal condescension. There was no question of removing his handcuffs. His escort examined the interior and then decided to ride in front with his colleagues. As soon as the doors were locked the van moved off at speed. Smyrna unsteadily attempted to wipe his nose first with the back of one hand and then the other. He stared at the new-comer's handcuffs with a curiosity that made him miss his own

54

nose. His mouth hung open. A fastidious expression appeared on the new prisoner's face.

—You're a dirty bugger aren't you.

A modish disc-jockey drawl had been superimposed on his local accent. The effect would have been comic but for the menacing stillness of his narrow head. It was held in some invisible vice of his own making. His eyes, pale and yet glinting dangerously, were also still beyond the grey tint of the thin convex lenses.

—I don't like dirty buggers near me. I can tell you that now. What do they call you?

Smyrna's jaw stretched out as he considered the quiet words addressed to him. Was this a new threat forming itself? Had his environment become totally hostile. The well-dressed prisoner was handcuffed after all. He was a man of slight build. He looked down unhappily at his own powerful arms and began once again to examine the bandages on his wrists.

—Smyrna, he said. Smyrna. That's what they call me.

—What's that for Christ's sake. Some bloody Welsh chapel, or something?

He bared the bottom of his immaculate teeth in an unfriendly smile.

—Now look here . . .

The minister felt obliged to intervene.

—You must understand that our young friend here isn't at all well. You can see for yourself.

The cold eyes shifted to examine the minister for the first time.

—Who the hell are you? His old Dad or something?

He directed the same question to Smyrna with the slightest nod towards the minister. He was amused by his own remarks.

—Your old dad, is he? Come for the ride?

The minister made an appeal for sociability.

—Now look here, he said. We are all in the same boat. In the same van anyway. Let us make an effort to get on together, and help each other.

The handcuffed man studied the minister with the absorbed but objective interest of an ornithologist examining a known if unfamiliar species in the wholly inappropriate habitat.

—How long you in for, Moses?

—A month. Twenty eight days that is.

The minister was prepared to be relaxed and jovial.

—Oh dearie me. That's a very long time isn't it? What about you snotty Smyrna?

—Eighteen months.

Smyrna's large head sank on his chest. His jaw began to work. In the depth of his misery he seemed unaware of a trickle of mucus that ran from his nostril over the edge of his upper lip.

—Wipe your snot, you dirty bugger.

The handcuffed prisoner's voice rose sharply to assert itself above the noise of the engine taking a hill in low gear.

—I bet you're one of those miserable sods who grind their bloody teeth in their sleep. Aren't you?

Smyrna smiled rather foolishly. He had no defence except to try and be friendly.

—How long you in for then?

He put the question with amiable innocence and waited patiently for an answer. A pulse began to beat visibly in the handcuffed man's tightened jaws.

—Nine.

He spoke at last, but so quietly Smyrna leaned forward as though he were about to complain he hadn't heard. One of the police escort shifted in his cramped seat to peer back at them through the steel bars. The scream of the engine subsided a little.

—Nine months did you say?

Smyrna was smiling inanely.

—Nine fucking years you snotty piece of crap. If they can hold me.

He lifted his handcuffed hands to the breast pocket of his smart suit and let them fall again.

—Here . . .

He was ordering Smyrna to extract a packet of cigarettes from the pocket. Smyrna glanced apprehensively at the broad backs of the policemen in front.

—Never mind them, snotty. When you're inside you do as I tell you. You may as well start now.

Smyrna was permitted a cigarette himself. He was instructed to sit alongisde his new master to enjoy it.

—You sit there mate, and then I won't have to bloody look at you.

Smyrna settled down, inhaling deeply and giggling. He blew on the end of the cigarette and pointed it at Mr. Ellis.

—He's a minister, he said.

—Is he now? Well, well. He should be sorry for us.

He held out his handcuffed wrists and nudged Smyrna to do the same. When he understood the order, Smyrna shook so much with silent giggles that he had difficulty in keeping his bandaged wrists level and close to the handcuffs.

—We make a pair. A pair of Jacks. Isn't that so, Snotty? a pair of Jacks.

Smyrna laughed delightedly. He let his arms drop but a glance from his new companion made him raise them again.

—What is it then. What is it you're in for?

The minister cleared his throat. He straightened his back.

—For refusing to buy my television licence, he said. On principle.

—Oh my God. One of them language fanatics. I tell you what I'd do, Moses, if I was in charge. I'd stick the bloody lot of you up against a wall—

—You don't understand, the minister said. I'm not blaming you. You've never had a chance to understand.

—Do you hear that?

The man in handcuffs elbowed Smyrna again to show him he could lower his arms if he wanted to since he had decided the joke was over.

—He's a fucking Welsh hero. That's what he is. In for twenty days and then out for a fucking laurel crown made of leeks. That's him. I tell you what we'll do, snotty. We'll be in the same cell tonight. And I won't be wearing my bracelets. How about knitting him a nice little crown of thorns?

Smyrna inhaled cigarette smoke to the bottom of his lungs and nodded gleefully.

57

Poems

Interim verdict

It is not necessary that you continue
You are not indispensable or absolute
Except for certain moments
When the sunlight
Is brushed by shadows of branches on the classroom wall
When light drops laughter
In that woman's eyes
And a damp wind girdles the tree trunk
And small sharp teeth sink
Into fruit that spreads its honey
Over little fingers
At such moments, prisoner,
Not recorded in the indictment

You may imagine if you will
That you are for ever
And that only in so far as you perceive do you exist
And that your existence is more and always more
Than the image of a victim
Racing towards the dark.

You shall continue. And continue for ever and ever.
Through you and never altogether without you
Others will go on stumbling through the mist
The fish will shudder in the deep-sea cold
The poet mutter, the insect shift under the cruel stone.

A tree waiting

A tree grows in its own time.
Stubborn and tender
Like caucasian miners, slaves of their devotion,
Roots crawl between buried rocks
Loyal not only to each other
But to their green offspring
Paying their fees
For many summer terms.

That is responsibility. Birds
By comparison are frivolous. They squat
In their foul nests preening their feathers
Twittering about their rights
Celebrating in a riot of repetition
Their seasonal behaviour. Why should we
Marvel at their navigational powers?

Roots have to do with a system
But they are also signatures
Of a covenant, substance
Of a love that is native
Growing in its own time and its own place.

Partial recall

Small as a top in the green garden
A boy fished for Time with a string and a broken stick
As if the breeze that stroked his cheek could harden
Or upstairs, after dark, the flame solidify upon its wick

White-kneed cap-crooked in the sepia photograph
Before the War that put the sun to flight
He climbed the limestone hill, hid behind the gorse
And came down with a vision and an appetite

His mother or the maid did their best to stifle
With green peas, potatoes, meat or fish
On willow-pattern plates and on the bench outside
The loyal terrier waited to lick the sticky dish.

Childhood is conviction. The seeds of magic.
There must be places where these things are stored
Like dust between the granary floorboards or
Those ink smudges left inside the roller towel
Behind the kitchen door

Enter the cave. There afternoons like bats
Hang black and leathern in the nets of Time
And on the sandy floor the dead in their dry hospice
Lie wrapped in soundless music line by line.

Two generations

i. The Father

Those who fight and win are entitled to their reward
The service in the old style
A villa in the pines with a view of the sea.

Sit on the balcony and watch the sunburnt boys
Pluck the cones on the fir tree
Watch the judas trees cast their enticing shadows
On the pink garden walls.

At ten thirty the chauffeur calls in uniform
It is time to be driven to the riding school
Above the lake there are yellow blooms
My wife rides side-saddle through the eucalyptus trees
The cook will do the shopping.

Tomorrow my friend returns from Mexico.
My broker rang from Brazil. That ivory horse
My son brought back from Hong-Kong.
Three nuns visit my wife in the afternoons
To perfect their grammar.
I ride up-country to see my bulls.
The young men line up in tight brown trousers
To prove their manhood. This writer chap said
We torment and expel our bulls
As if they were reincarnated Moors . . . and I say 'we'
As if I were one of the natives.

No life is perfect. My wife makes friends
I feel obliged to hate. I walk in the cork forest
Until they are gone and think of the riding school
And my controlling interest
And worry a little about the country's affairs.

The Russians are inefficient. That is a comfort.
Maybe the Chinese will gobble them up
Before they finish us off.
Frankly it's machines I'm afraid of . . .
I won't allow them on the place.

In the evening let the maid appear
And circulate the oval table with her second load of French
cuisine.
Let the old priest fall asleep before the fire
Let my wife talk of exiled kings and queens,

There are generations yet unborn
Who will admire my style and my reward
If I can make it last . . .
If they build that hotel block
To overlook my garden I tell you this
I'll blow it up.

ii. The Eldest Son

'There's nowhere like London! London's the place!
Admit it!' He nibbles his lip with excitement
Pushes his hair about and buys his paper.
It's going to rain, but he wears no mac
There are holes in his shoes and three cheque-books in his
pocket.

The headlines are in his hands. 'Do you know
I stood here once about a year ago on a very bright morning
Outside Hamley's watching the buses and taxis
And the thousands of faces flowing up and down
When I realised . . . I hadn't noticed before . . . A man in dark
glasses

Standing right by my side. And do you know who it was?
Yes! Yes! It was Him! Radiant with promise
Perfumed with success. I noticed his shoes you know
Incredibly ritzy and a gold watch on his wrist and hair on his
                                                            forearms
Made for eternity or Pharaoh's tomb

I said 'Hello' and he smiled. He didn't take off his sun-glasses
But he smiled alright. In fact he said 'Hello Buddy!'
I wanted to ask him without seeming oafish
If he'd heard of our venture, our Big Thing you know
And could I tell him a little about it.
Just as I made my first noise a chauffeur-driven Bentley
Drew up like a visiting ghost and whisked him away
Back to the Gods I suppose, those Elysian fields,
That charismatic platform between the stars!

That's London you see, anything can happen.
Governments fall and here you are in the same street
Reading about it! Great men die
And you stand here inhaling the perturbation
Sharing the tension with every heart that hurries by.

You can't be informed by a garden. Or buy newspapers from
                                                            trees.

I'll wait for the next edition. It's got to come out . . . It's got
                                                            to!
You stand here long enough and History becomes
Someone you've met. There are shreds of wealth in the air
And kingly music, fortunes won and lost
Love reflected in every window and in the sky
Images of scandalous women elevated
By our breath, their backs their buttocks their breasts
Preserved in electric milk and all day long
Although *you* cannot hear it, every thing is singing.'

Brân

i.

Calm as green apples
Under the spider's thread
The kingdom of Brân

Brân
Emblem of one island
The strongest man
A giant armed
Blessed with gentleness

Bendigeidfrân

As a rock that tames
The unruly seas
He ruled
His mouth
A hall of justice

He commanded first
Himself
His eyes
Were smiling doors

There was so much strength
In his arms
He held them still
And like the sun
He kept his distance

Under his royal shadow
Houses sheltered
Ships sailed
Into harbour
Between his feet

Unafraid
While his aura
Lit
The western sky.

ii.

From this rock
That He has made my throne

I court the beauty of the western sea
And the setting sun
I see my brother's chariot
Crossing a plain of water

And the flowers of another kingdom
Flourishing under the crystal sea

Sea horses glisten as far as my eye can see
And among them fruit and flowers, a stream of honey
To make the sweet mead of the second world

In my stillness
Both my kingdoms flourish
The salmon leap from the womb
Of the white sea
And the animals of God
Walk unharmed among the water and the wolves.

Poetry, prison and propaganda

A good poem is like a machine that defies the test to destruction. Each new reader avidly digs his teeth into it like some forest rodent looking for the ultimate warm hole where he can hibernate at least as long as the winter of his personal discontent. There is only one sun in the sky, but a good poem creates an alternative sunrise. It borrows light and colour for our private use from a galaxy to which we do not belong. A good poem has something for everybody: even for the most secretive and dangerous of predators, the translator.

The Welsh language is so well supplied with good poems it seems unbelievable that it should be in the slightest danger of extinction. (It is a well known fact that good poems purify and preserve languages. That has always been part of their social function.) Of course there are politicians who for their own dark reasons secretly long and actively work for its demise on road signs and elsewhere: but there are also editors of anthologies and journalists with literary yearnings who love to lean forward and whisper in the reader's ear that if the truth were known four fifths of the population of 'this little country of ours' do not understand a word of their national language. It should occur to them more often that this means four fifths of the population are being denied their most precious birthright; unimpeded access to that reservoir of good poems that exists for the dual purpose of mental health and quenching the thirst of the soul. (If a consistent Welsh socialist theory could be conjured into existence, with or without the assistance of Tom Nairn, at this late hour, the achievement of Aneurin Bevan as Minister to the physical health of the British Isles should inspire our more brilliant Labour politicians to consider the creation of a Welsh Ministry of Mental Health that would dispense poetry in the native tongue like aspirin on National Health prescription. "Go home and learn 'Y Llwynog' off by heart, and come back to see me in a week's time . . .") It is hard to understand how so many who pretend to a love of literature and the practice of literary art can continue to excuse themselves from the obligation of learning not merely the language of their forefathers but also the vitally necessary linguistic landscape where good poems designed for their particular needs naturally flourish.

Good poems have the strange quality of appearing to have existed as long as the language in which they live. And yet this must be an illusion. A poetic tradition, no matter how ancient and august, cannot produce good poems of itself. It may very well be one of the oldest extant literary traditions in Europe,—if not the oldest: but it could do nothing without the impact of the individual talent. The relation between the seed and the soil can always be analysed in great detail; but as in logic and mathematics there is a residue of mystery; and not the least in the Welsh situation of the twentieth century is the flowering of so many individual talents at the very time when the stage managers of history and their lethargic agents in the Welsh community had the language boxed up in an iron lung specially designed to serve as a coffin.

All these individual talents were politically active. In fact poets in the Welsh language had not been so politically active since the fifteenth century. And yet there is little propaganda in their poetry. It could be argued of course that the twentieth century has produced a civilisation that is hostile to poets in general, giving them the straight choice of the garret or the grave. But this does not seem to be the case with what the late W. J. Gruffydd used to call "our neighbours the English". If you write enough good poems in English you still stand a good chance of an O.M. in old age. Even in bustling America, Robert Frost had an honoured place at the Kennedys' Instant Round Table. Off hand I cannot think of a major English poet of the last hundred years serving a prison sentence. (Unless someone wishes to count Oscar Wilde: to which the immediate reply has to be that he was Anglo-Irish suffering as it were for Anglo-pederasty rather than Irish politics). However, a prison sentence is something that the three poets translated below have in common. Since all three were brought up in respectable Welsh non-conformist homes at a time when Wales of the White Gloves was proudly claimed to be the most law abiding corner of the British Empire, this is a phenomenon that requires extended explanation. But the explanation would need to be done in Welsh and the reader if curious enough would need to learn that language to follow it: which brings us back once again to the delights of the linguistic landscape. As it is, the reader will be obliged to take my word if I say that since Thomas Gwyn Jones there has not been a Welsh poet of real consequence who has not been faced at some point or other in the course of his career with the prospect of a prison sentence.

Gwenallt found himself in prison before he found himself a poet. He had joined the I.L.P. before the age of seventeen. His father was a steelworks furnaceman and a deacon in Soar Calvinistic Methodist Chapel at Pontardawe. Always his parents spoke of the Carmarthenshire countryside of their origins as an Eden which they had been forced to leave and to which they longed to return. In 1917 as a conscientious objector on socialist grounds, he was imprisoned first in Wormwood Scrubs and then in Dartmoor. There can be little doubt from the evidence in his autobiographical novel, *Plasau'r Brenin* that it was the power of the family myth of Carmarthenshire rural life that kept the young man's sanity during the two year sentence. The poem *Dartmoor* published in 1942, shows how vividly the experience could be relived almost a quarter of a century later. This English adaptation of the poem came to light while moving house recently. It is extremely free in more than one sense since it presumes to include an invocation of the poet. However since he was the first poet that I read and understood in the Welsh original, this might be excused. It seems to have been made in the middle forties, at some time when the cyclical need for hibernation was making itself felt.

Dartmoor

Bars burn again across your eyes. Doors
Clang upon your ears
Lags, lunatics, sow and reap their sighs
Break acres of remorse on those cold moors.

August you saw spread heavy sunsets
Like slaughter, blood into pools and ditches.
November came distributing mists
Imprisoning the prison. The nights belonged to witches.

You heard them. The congregation of the damned
Assembled and in session with their dogs
Their screech owls and their endless cries
Of pain and guilt. Shapes writing in the fog:

But in your cell you gripped your necklace of goodness, your
                                                    lucky charm,
The blue river Tywi winding between farm and farm.

When Gwenallt was in Dartmoor, Saunders Lewis was in
Salonika: a Captain with the South Wales Borderers, he had
been wounded in France and transferred to work with British
Intelligence in Greece. As far as is known, and so unlike his
friend David Jones, Saunders Lewis has never written an extended creative work based on his experience of war. One explanation could well be that his whole life has been a continuing
battle for the country to which he pledged his allegiance while
still in the trenches at Loos.

When *Haf Bach Mihangel 1941* was written in the autumn of
1941 the outcome of the second world war was still in doubt. In
mid-September Kiev had fallen to the Germans. In the vivid
little diaries of Ambrose Bebb the entry for Medi 19, 1941
begins '. . . The splendour of this September continues, school
visits . . . To be out in the morning in sight of the fields, the
aftermath and the stubble, and all the miracles of this month of
masterpieces . . . and then to open the newspaper,—the messenger from hell. Kiev has fallen'.

While the fate of Europe hung in the balance, in Wales the
strings of 'national' power were being quietly transferred from
the last remnants of the Lloyd George Liberal network into the
hands of a new generation of tacit supporters of the Labour
Party. In charge of this silent operation was the grey eminence
of the period, Dr. Thomas Jones C.H. The former secretary of
the Imperial Cabinet was a past-master of the arcane arts of manipulation. The position of Saunders Lewis, the former Presi-
dent of Plaid Cymru, was somewhat more exposed: sacked
from the university; hated with equal intensity by the old and
the new Establishments; suspected by the chapels and churches;
reviled by the fashionable fellow travellers and armchair
Marxists as a Catholic and pillar of Reaction; liable at any time
to be sent back to prison for speaking his mind with too great a
degree of frankness and independence in his weekly article in *Y
Faner*, "Cwrs y Byd", a title by the way, taken from the prose
masterpiece of the early eighteenth century (Gweledigaeth y

74

Bard Cwsg—'The Vision of the Sleeping Bard'); our poet would have been justified in complaining somewhat, albeit in gentle numbers, of his own wearisome condition. Instead, this poem is a prayer for ordinary simple folk in time of war. And to whom is the intercession made? Michael the archangel, prominent in the Jewish, Christian and Mohammedan religions as the commander in the celestial war where Lucifer was finally defeated. (The avid reader, well versed in his Lewis will remember the speech of Colonel von Hofacker in *Brad* . . . 'That is the meaning of Hitler. He carries the mark of the Archangel of Chaos, the supernatural will and power to destroy, the Archenemy of man and God'.) This same Michael in Wales inherited the shrines and sites of the ancient Celtic religion: so that when we invoke Michael and all the angels somewhere among the cloud of witnesses the ghostly shadows of the ancient celtic pantheon are also moving.

St Michael's Little Summer 1941

Spring came and went with little sunlight
To pick out the blue flash of the swallow under the bridge;
Nursed by the warm wet summer
Green shoots sprouted in the August corn:
With the mail so slow from Egypt, from Singapore
Women held their ears closer to a voice in a box . . .
A terrible slaughter in Russia I should think . . .
And the rain dripped like worry day after day
On backs bent with that eloquence beyond words:
That was the war in our village,
An assembly in the distance, a wall of doom approaching,
A black threat hiding the lightning:
And on the mantlepiece the English voice in the box
Our tiny share of mass communication
Announcing and pronouncing
While the postman mutters his own news from door to door
With names that are nearer, Cardiff . . . Swansea . . . Our
South,
Retailing unspecified fear; faces, tongues are strangers;
Who can think, who can speak his mind
Except that confident voice in the box boasting

Our navy, *our* airforce, and we more hesitant than ever
To believe that we are we
As we move like a people under a spell
From the yard to the field
Where our hands may feel things solid as old certainties
And other centuries
In the August rain.

But the wind turned. The early morning mist
Was scattered by the slow power of a royal sun.
There was a breadth of afternoon and a sunset of streaming
banners
Before the Great Bear closed his arms around the night sky;
There was a loading of carts in the cornfield
And in the orchard the dew glittered
On the still gossamer that hung between green apples;
This was Michael's gift, a hill to restore us,
A sanctuary of summer haze in late September
Balm before winter, before the testing time, before the dark
Before weighing anchor and sailing like Ulysses
Beyond the last headland of the living:
'O Brothers, do not avoid the brief vigil
The last experience, what remains for us to learn
Of the splendour and misery of this world . . .'
And Dante saw him with Diomede, two in one fire.

Michael, lover of mountains pray in our hills
Michael, friend of the maimed and the sick, remember
Wales.

Waldo Williams was getting on when he went to prison in
1960 and 1961 for refusing to pay his Income Tax as part of his
antiwar protest which had begun as far back as the Korean
War. Of the three poets, so actively engaged in politics, he was,
in one sense, the only true extremist. Gwenallt's early socialism
was part of a view of the world now common to the overwhelm-
ing majority of the Welsh people. Saunders Lewis was a prophet of moderation obliged to live his long life in an age of dizzy
expectation; an age of fantasies lulled either by war machines or

76

the mechanised profit motive operating the productive appetite of an advanced industrial society; an age in fact of licensed immoderation. For his part, Waldo Williams took the line of uncompromising rejection. Perhaps to a man of such mystical and innocent temperament, it was not so difficult to take on the rough robes of the hermit. If it is a choice, he seems to be saying, between the obscenities of Belsen and Hiroshima and cold subsistence in an unheated cave, give me the latter. As is so often the case with gentle mystics, there is something frightening and yet exhilarating in the ruthless way he applies his own logic to his own self. His is the language of the Simone Weil who sorrowfully rejected Marxist doctrine after a courageous career of protest and went in search of God. This quality of 'Holy Simplicity' makes his poetry particularly difficult to translate. He has the temerity to speak of eternal things in the language of a child. This seems to be still possible in Welsh; or at least it was up to the time of Waldo's death. The poem makes full use of the succinct and uniquely Welsh verbnoun to achieve much of its effect.

Pa Beth yw Dyn?

What is living? Finding a great hall
Inside a cell.
What is knowing? One root
To all the branches.

What is believing? Holding out
Until relief comes.
And forgiving? Crawling through thorns
To the side of an old foe.

What is singing? Winning back
The first breath of creation:
And work should be a song
Made of wheat or wood.

What is statecraft? Something
Still on all fours.
And defence of the realm?
A sword thrust in a baby's hand.

What is being a nation? A talent
Springing in the heart.
And love of country? Keeping house
Among a cloud of witness.

What is this world to the great powers?
A circle turning.
And to the lowly of the earth?
A cradle rocking.

One final gloss for the dual purpose of underlining the harsh
fact of untranslatability and the urgent need of the reader to
acquire the language. Of the phrase, *Cadw tŷ mewn cwmwl
tystion*, the philosopher J. R. Jones had this to say in his book *Ac
Onide* . . . 'In this phrase I see a clear picture of the kind of thing
I mean when I speak of being aware of the past and of the relationship of the past to life as we are living it. 'Cadw tŷ'—this
means daily life, housekeeping, earning our daily bread,—the
'economic' world in general, since we understand the original
meaning of that word 'oikonomia'—the science and the craft of
housekeeping . . . this is what the whole of mankind has in
common, the necessity of a working life. How then can our life
claim to have an unique and separate national quality? How do
we follow our routine daily tasks in the secure knowledge that
what we do is part of the life flow of our particular nation? No
doubt our alloted space gives part of the answer—the theatre of
our effort. On this territory, on the earth of our country,
together we keep house. But the Past must also be an integral
part of the answer. You are keeping house surrounded by a
cloud of witnesses, not witnesses of flesh and blood, but a *cloud*
of witnesses—witnesses in the mind, in the language you speak,
witnesses from the past. We know of course where Waldo
picked up the phrase. After the roll-call of the great figures of
the nation's past, Abraham, Isaac, Jacob, Moses, the author of
the Letter to the Hebrews addresses those who remain "Where-
fore seeing we also are compassed about with so great a cloud of
witnesses, let us lay aside every weight, and the sin which doth
so easily beset us, and let us run with patience the race that is set
before us . . ." The cloud of witnesses of a nation are the generations of her history . . . The athlete runs the course under the

eyes of the crowd, in the arena . . . The line of verse invites the reader to live and work in the arena of the vanishing present under the watchful eye of past history: this generation is not abandoned, not cut off, because the eyes of the past are watching, in, outside and above the words . . . Witnesses of what? To the fact of identity which is even more important than the result of the race. The past functions as a special part of memory. Everyone knows how memory and remembering re-assure the individual of his existence. Loss of memory is a crippling psychological condition . . . Only in remembered history is there evidence that can tell us truly who exactly we are . . .' The analysis continues for several pages. It is informa-tion of the first importance, but not fully to be understood without reading the whole book in the original.

Every language has its own magic. This means that every language has its own source of power. For example, a good poem can transform sorrow into joy, as in the case of these three poems in their original form. This is magic, on a level of experience far beyond eloquence. In the old days of cheerful hypocrisy and labyrinthine national double-think, platform orators described Welsh as the language of heaven: this happily relieved them of the obligation of using it properly on earth. But there was a minute grain of truth in their hackneyed hyperbole. Poems can be prayers composed by lunatics or saints for fervent repetition by the generality of sinners.

The phenomenon of 'Culture Shift' from which Wales has been suffering for the last sixty years is a terrible thing: as awesome as an earthquake or a tempest and more damaging in its lasting effect. No doubt it is a world wide phenomenon and many educated Welshmen, well trained in the sheltered art of passive observation, are happy to argue that the whole process has gone too far to be reversed. Alas, this comfortable argument is never available to poets, or for that matter to their genuinely avid readers. The force that helps to produce good poems is part of the creative energy that will lead humanity out of the despair of the dark wood. Save Welsh, Cymry, and you may help to save the world.

Arnold in wonderland

On a Saturday in August in the year 1864, Mr. Matthew Arnold, Professor of Poetry at the University of Oxford and Her Majesty's Inspector of Schools, sat in number ten, St. George's Crescent, Llandudno, writing holiday letters to relatives and friends. The date, as always, is very relevant. In the dim caves of Mount Helicon where history is being constantly rewritten, dates are like glow worms that provide the weavers with the only source of light. But so is the address. Middle class and robustly anglophile. St. George's Crescent. An architectural scimitar lying across the dragon's throat.

The distinguished letter writer is forty two and in a state of pleasurable excitement: in Llandudno, on the Welsh coast, there was a distinct possibility that his poetic career, that seemed so ominously complete, could be resumed: the visionary gleam could be returning. The Inspector of Schools, braced and refreshed by the Celtic breeze, would turn once more to the 'grand business of modern poetry, that moral interpretation, from an independent point of view, of man and the world'.

'The poetry of the Celtic race', he wrote to his mother, 'and its names of places quite overpowers me and it will be long before Tom forgets the line, "Hear from thy grave, great Taliesin, hear", from Gray's Bard, since I have repeated it a hundred times a day on our excursions'.

After all his mother was Cornish. Her maiden name was Penrose, a word surely cognate with that Penrhos through which he walked with his brother Tom on several of his excursions. Being half Celtic had become a stimulating concept. Perhaps it brought relief to the intensity of moral earnestness, labelled Teutonic by his father and headmaster, deeply instilled in childhood and youth and then reinforced by a mature sense of mission.

'Then also', he writes to Lady de Rothschild, 'I have a great penchant for the Celtic races, with their melancholy and unprogressiveness'.

It is never difficult to trace the sources of Matthew Arnold's ideas and enthusiasms. He made little attempt to conceal them. His stance as an advocate of high culture and arbiter of literary taste in England did not depend on originality. The driving force of his message lay in its concern with, and application to, the English situation. His business was with the refinement of the condition of middle class success. History was clearly in the process of delivering the wide world into the hands of the English. England was the new Rome. A new form of Empire had come into being apparently as much by accident as by design. Such rude vigour and crude success had to be provided with a higher purpose. By some divine accident which a more superstitious age would have called a miracle, the imperiousness of the Norman, the honesty of the Saxon, the thoroughness of the Teuton and the Titanism of the Celt had been combined to create the potential of a new race of supermen. The Church of England, his father had already pointed out, needed to be made more flexible, to accommodate wider concepts. A place had to be made for the drive and dedication of Dissent, for the re-organisation of Education, for the fruits of Science and the Power that came with extended Trade and Knowledge. Dr. Arnold of Rugby was an opponent of Disestablishment for his own reasons.

> The Church, never disestablished but dedicated to England . . . of all human ties that to our country is the highest and most sacred: and England to a true Englishman ought to be dearer than the peculiar forms of the Church of England.

In that mild way which in the end merely reinforces the fact of apostolic succession, Matthew Arnold had rebelled against his father. For him, C of E, meant the Culture of England. An improved breed of English poets and men of letters would eventually replace the old ministry. An elevated culture would be capable not only of providing a 'criticism of Life': it would also replace dogma to become the true source of righteousness and personal morality. But there was a great deal of hard work to be done. Wordsworth, Keats, Shelley, Byron, Tennyson, Browning, talented as they were, had not succeeded in lifting English verse up to the Olympian levels of the work of his hero Goethe. Until the whole body of modern English writing could be seen to combine the virtues and excel the output of German and French, the language could not take off and provide the best parts of the nations of the earth with the appropriate cultural extension of universal practical Christianity.

A man with a mission has earned his rest and he has a right to

relax on his holidays. Reading *La poesie des races celtiques* by
Renan, Arnold had learned that this obscure body of poetry was
characterised by spirituality, melancholy and a heightened
awareness of nature. Arnold had no knowledge of Welsh or of
any Celtic language. But the poet in him quickly overpowered
the educator. As he stood barefooted and bare headed *ar ben y
Gogarth*, that most conspicuous of headlands, did he not feel
within himself the exquisite sensations of spirituality, sweet
melancholy and a heightened awareness of nature? True his feet
were bare for mundane Teutonic reasons. He had a blister on
his big toe as a result of too much excited tramping about on
Wordsworthian 'excursions'. The place is now the Great
Orme's Head and the site of cafes, overhead railways, litter
bins, and funfairs, but in 1864 the coastline of Wales could still
provide a poet in any language with the feeling that he could be
treading on sacred ground. Bays, inlets, rocky shores, promon-
tories and deserted beaches combined with the generous sea to
provide an infinite variety of symphonic sunsets.

> At last one turns around and looks westward. Everything is
> changed. Over the mouth of the Conway and its sands is the eternal
> softness and mild light of the west; the low line of mystic Anglesey,
> the precipitious Penmaenmawr, and the group of Carnedd Llewelyn
> and Carnedd David, and their brethren fading away, hill behind
> hill, in an aerial haze, make the horizon; between the fort of Pen-
> maenmawr and the bending coast of Anglesey, the sea, a silver
> stream, disappears one knows not whither. On this side, Wales—
> Wales, where the past still lives, where every place has its tradition,
> every name its poetry, and where the people, the genuine people,
> still knows this past, this tradition, this poetry, and lives with it and
> clings to it; while, alas, the prosperous Saxon on the other side, the
> invader from Liverpool and Birkenhead, has long ago forgotten his.

The prose style is still beguiling. In an easy urbane fashion, it
exercises its own authority. It is an active world of assertion
from which all coarseness and vulgarity has been excluded. It
has the strength of concern and the delicacy of a cultivated
aesthetic sense. And it has more. For the purpose of these four
lectures on *The Study of Celtic Literature*, Professor Arnold has
donned druidical robes. The Order of his own making. As
befits a poet who is attempting to synthesise a modern mythology, his utterance is reaching out towards incantation. To

achieve his effects he is prepared to pay the price of over-simplification. The levy is not onerous. In dealing with such an obscure subject, accuracy is not important: the effect is all. Somehow or other, the haughty Philistines of England must be made aware of the Celtic species expiring on the westward peri-meter of the world's most advanced and prosperous state. Here was the son of Arnold of Rugby, 'That Teuton of Teutons, the Celt-hating Dr. Arnold', telling the world that the despised and dejected Celts still had something valuable to offer.

> When I was young, I was taught to think of Celt as separated by an impassable gulf from Teuton: my father in particular was never weary of contrasting them: he insisted much oftener on the separa-tion between us and them than on the separation between us and any other race in the world.

The central argument of Arnold's message of reconciliation between conquered Celt and all-conquering Saxon was some-thing he declared to be scientific.

> The Celt's claims towards having his genius and its works fairly treated as objects of scientific investigation, the Saxon can hardly reject, when these claims are urged simply on their own merits, and are not mixed up with extraneous pretentions which jeopardise them.

An adroit manipulation of syntax conjures up the illusion of an atmosphere of scientific detachment. At the same time, the impersonal calm, the judicial manner, the authoritative concern for the English commonwealth, underline the fact that the Celts in the manner of tramps, gipsies, poachers, disrespect-ful labourers and other elements from the unstable sediment of an otherwise well-ordered society, are up before the bench. In the end, sentence will have to be passed. The most pressing question at issue is which set of laws should be applied in this case. From his chosen stance as judge-advocate, there is no doubt in Arnold's mind.

> What the French call the *science des origines*—the science of origins,—a science which is at the bottom of all real knowledge of the actual world, and which is every day growing in interest and importance—is very incomplete without a thorough critical account of the Celts and their genius, language and literature.

In order that no one should doubt his good intentions, in his introduction to the lectures, Arnold gallantly defends the hapless Welsh and their Eisteddfod from the blunt, blistering and blustering verdict of The Times Newspaper.

> The Welsh language is the curse of Wales . . . An Eisteddfod is one of the most mischievous and selfish pieces of sentimentalism which could possibly be perpetrated. It is simply a foolish interference with the natural progress of civilisation and prosperity . . . Not only the energy and power, but the intelligence and music of Europe have come mainly from Teutonic sources, and this glorification of every-thing Celtic, if it were not pedantry, would be sheer ignorance. The sooner all Welsh specialities disappear from the face of the earth the better.

Arnold is opposed to the harshness and the brutal frankness: the unacceptable face of Anglican uniformity and Teutonic intolerance. What he offers is a softer approach to the first of the final solutions based on the science of origins which so deeply stirred the imagination and even the 'imaginative reason' of the men of the nineteenth century and provided the twentieth with its most terrifying popular myth. He cannot help being sorry for the Celts particularly 'the quiet, peaceable Welsh'.

> . . . his land is a province and his history petty, and his Saxon sub-duers scout his speech as an obstacle to civilisation, and the echo of all its kindred in other lands is growing every day fainter and more feeble: gone in Cornwall, going in Brittany and the Scotch Highlands, going too in Ireland and there above all, the badge of the beaten race, the property of the vanquished.

That summer of sixty four, the Eisteddfod pitched its tent in Llandudno. Professor Arnold's little boys were disappointed when they discovered it was not a circus. The professor himself, expecting too much from a Bardic Congress conducted in a lan-guage he could not understand, was disappointed to discover that it was. The Gorsedd was held in the open air. The weather was bad. The speeches were long. The presiding bard was got up in some absurd costume. Inside the tent things were no better. The back seats where the Welsh should have been seated were nearly empty. The front seats were occupied by Saxons who came there from curiosity, not enthusiasm. And when a

87

speech was made in English, powerful as it was, by a nonconformist divine, he inevitably spoilt his case by overstating it.
His eloquence was given a stony Teutonic response.

'The whole performance on that particular morning, was incurably lifeless'.

The Arnold family's diversions during their Llandudno stay
were not confined to romantic 'excursions' or attending Eisteddfodau. As he wrote to his sister when he mentioned spend-
ing three and a half hours on the Great Orme in bare feet . . .
'There are one or two people here'.

By this he means not the Saxon hordes he saw swarming in
from Liverpool, or the natives, those obscure descendants of the
myth-making Celts, selling vegetables and hiring donkeys to
the prosperous invaders. He means the social life of his own
kind: the privileged members of the middle class connected with
the aristocracy, with the Church of England, with Oxford colleges, with government circles and less openly perhaps with
commerce.

'There are one or two people here: the liddells, with whom
we dined; the scudmore stanhopes, him I slightly knew at oxford; the dean of chichester, a clergyman or two, who have
called'.

The Liddells, of course, were the family of the Dean of Christ
Church, Liddell of Liddell and Scott, the Greek Lexicon that
was as much a pillar of English public school education as Dr.
Arnold's Rugby reformations. Among 'the clergymen or two'
was the Reverend Charles Lutwidge Dodgson, lecturer and
tutor in mathematics at Christ Church. It is not unreasonable
to conjecture that he may have deserted the West Shore to look
in with clear-eyed curiosity at the proceedings of the Eisteddd-
fod. And the three little girls could have accompanied him: Lor-
inda Charlotte, Edith and Alice. As far as I know there is no
record of their reactions. The language barrier was unsur-
mountable. They must have returned to the West Shore to continue listening to the Walrus and the Carpenter. Alas, the pre-
adolescent wonderland was not available to the Welsh. Like the
oysters in the poem they were scheduled for polite but firm
extinction.

The Eisteddfod existed to celebrate the antiquity and honour
of the Welsh language, in what could only appear the most

harmless manner. It is not easy to discover Matthew Arnold's deepest objections to the Eisteddfod. He states that he found the proceedings at Llandudno 'incurably lifeless', yet in a letter to Hugh Owen he becomes quite fulsome.

> When I see the enthusiasm these Eisteddfods can awaken in your whole people, and then think of the tastes, the literature, the amusements, of our own lower middle class, I am filled with admiration for you. It is a consoling thought and one which history allows us to entertain, that nations disinherited of political success may yet leave their mark on the world's progress, and contribute powerfully to the civilisation of mankind.

This would appear to be a remarkable insight on the part of an intelligent foreigner into the true nature of the institution, and its origin. Iolo Morganwg like Lewis Carroll had a passion for literary anonymity. Carroll wished to forge a world of innocence out of his obsessive observation of little girls between the ages of eight and twelve. Iolo's forgeries were more ambitious. He wanted nothing less than to restore the supremacy of the Cambro-British. The Gorsedd and the revived and enlarged Eisteddfod were the creation of a private patriotism of demented proportions. This Welsh Jacobin and Unitarian created a necessary institution for the unprecedented expansion of Welsh consciousness that occurred in the first half of the nineteenth century. The Welsh were as hungry for identity as they were for religion. But Arnold writes of the Celt that . . . 'his speech is growing every day fainter and more feeble: gone in Cornwall, going in Brittany, and the Scotch Highlands, going too in Ireland . . .'

Going. Going. Going. This is the language of the auctioneer, rather than that of the literary critic. A sale of remnants is afoot and the auctioneer from Oxford, is anxious to persuade his Saxon clientele that there is something among the job-lot that is worth buying as well as burying. We cannot tell whether it is wishful thinking or a love of masterful generalisation that plays Arnold false. As far as the Welsh language was concerned, he could not have been more wrong. Unlike Cornish, Gaelic, or Breton, Welsh in the mid-nineteenth century was expanding more rapidly than ever before in History. The Eisteddfod with all its trappings was only one external manifestation of this expansion. It was to be encountered in Chicago, Philadelphia,

Cape Town, London, Sydney as well as in Llandudno. The Welsh rather like the Jews, sober and relatively prosperous, full of pretensions and those hated 'particularities', were irritatingly everywhere, carrying their language and their institutions with them.

There was a sound economic basis for this growth. Unlike Ireland and the Scottish Highlands, Wales in the nineteenth century was not ravaged by famine or depopulation. The industrial valleys of the South, and industry in the North (and that extension of Wales into Merseyside and Lancashire which gave us David Lloyd George and Saunders Lewis and gave them Selwyn Lloyd and Enoch Powell) were well able to absorb the population explosion. With the Welsh, religious and political motives remained as powerful as the drive for economic improvement. If Matthew Arnold had stayed long enough on the Great Orme's Head, with or without his boots on, he would have seen the first ship of yet another Welsh exodus—no chosen People are worthy of the title without this chapter in their story—the converted tea-clipper *Mimosa*, just avoiding the rocks off 'mystic Anglesey' on her way to an exclusively Welsh wonderland in South America. The 'Mimosa' was their 'Mayflower'.

Perhaps Arnold was not so unaware of the rising tide of Welshness after all. The trouble with the language was not that it was going, but that it was stubbornly refusing to go. On either side of the Atlantic the congregations of the dissenting chapels were growing larger from one revival to another. The princes of the pulpit who had once governed this world-wide Welsh commonwealth with as firm a hand as Dr. Arnold's at Rugby, had been obliged to bow to the popular desire for a wider culture and declare the Eisteddfod at least as respectable as the *Cornhill Magazine*. The occasional touch of royal patronage made it easy to conceal the republican and radical origin of Iolo's fancies under the Eisteddfodic robes.

But Professor Arnold was not easily deceived by such superficial symptoms. He recognised a dangerous disease and prescribed a remedy. While he waited in bare feet on the Great Orme's Head, the inevitable spark from heaven fell.

I must say I quite share the opinion of my brother Saxons as to the practical inconvenience of perpetuating the speaking of Welsh.

'Practical inconvenience' still has a contemporary ring about it. The language of government does not easily change. (It sounds equally well in the accent of Oxford or Tonypandy.) 'Perpetuating the speaking of Welsh' is more characteristically nineteenth century, it smacks clearly of the 'Welsh Not':

the change must come and its accomplishment is a mere affair of time. The sooner the Welsh language disappears . . . the better; the better for England, the better for Wales itself.

At last the nature of the sacrifice has been indicated, together with its true purpose. 'The moral interpretation', 'The independent point of view', has been transformed into an irrevocable judgement and the romantic practitioner of the grand business of modern poetry is suddenly transformed on that windy afternoon in Llandudno, somewhat in the manner of a Hollywood Dr. Jekyll, into a relentless Benthamite. Welsh was a totally unsatisfactory appliance of communication because it had never been used by Mr. Jeremy Bentham or learnt by Mr. Matthew Arnold. It had made and was making an inadequate contribution to those utilitarian twin ideals of Progress and Success. It was no good for England, and therefore no good for Wales. It was insufficiently useful. If it was not useful, it could never be virtuous. If it was not virtuous, much merit could be gained by discarding it. Ministers of Education (as it turns out Mr. Arnold's brother-in-law *is* the Minister of Education in 1870) must use the Elementary Schools to hammer Welsh out and English in, and 'hammer it harder and harder'. Arnold's phrase evokes the celluloid image of Mr. Hyde with his top hat on and his cloak flying, hammering away with his walking cane at the unconscious body of the faded prostitute lying on the pavement. Between punctuation marks he rushes back to the laboratory and swallows a draught of the restoring fluid before continuing in the more measured tones of the literary critic ready once more to do battle on behalf of culture and high art against the ranks of Philistia. The restoring fluid, we may guess, is by Taliesin. Three drops. Those oft repeated invocations have not been made in vain.

'Hear from thy grave, great Taliesin, hear!'

Since the Reverend Dodgson was in the vicinity he may have found a bottle with the words DRINK ME beautifully printed on it in large English letters. There should be no mistake in signs of this sort. It was not marked poison and it was perfectly safe to drink it. And that was how our hero first tasted *Celtic Magic*.

Those of us who wonder how our grandparents came so easily to abandon their native language, and our natural heritage, at a time when it seemed to be prospering as never before, should consider the correspondence between Matthew Arnold and that ubiquitous Benthamite busybody, Hugh Owen. In the eighteen sixties Welsh dissent, Welsh speaking dissent, was poised to become an independent political force. Arnold with his life-long fear of Irish Fenianism could not have been unaware of this. And the Welsh at that time were organised in a way that was still beyond the capability of the Irish. Throughout the first half of the nineteenth century chapels had been going up at the rate of one a fortnight. At first Welsh dissenters had been content to confine themselves to theology. Unlike the *science of origins* that so took Arnold's fancy, theology was an exacting discipline. In their own language this people possessed on a popular level an extraordinary ideological net-work and a language which supported such a variety of newspapers, magazines, encyclopaedias, pamphlets, and books could hardly be described as dying. Every chapel and every meeting house was a potential political cell. Arnold understood this. As an Inspector of Schools it was part of his duty to be aware of any hidden threat to the uniformity of the State. He was as much devoted as his father had been to the concept of the State as a God-ordained, mystical, and sacred entity. From Hegel they derived that notable Teutonic ideal that States and the Laws of States, were nothing less than Religion manifesting itself in the relations of the actual world.

> The fusion of all the inhabitants of these islands into one homogenous, English-speaking whole . . . the swallowing up of separate provincial nationalities, is a consummation towards which the natural course of things irresistibly tends.

Arnold's elevation of the concept of culture can be interpreted as an attempt to extend an Hegelian reverence for the State. This would account for his implacable hostility to the Welsh language on the one hand and his eagerness on the other, to make Celtic magic easily accessible for the enrichment of English civilisation. The Welsh language was an unreliable and volatile spirit which could give too much life to Welsh dissent and encourage an endless succession of disruptive and even seditious movements. Working class movements, trade unionism, manifestations of rural and industrial discontent all had their origins among chapel people. Disestablishment of the Church of England in England which had caused his father so much concern was hardly more than an academic issue: in Ireland and in Wales, provincial nationalisms tainted religious controversy. A separate language was an ever present threat of separatist intentions.

But Arnold need not have worried. There was absolutely no cause for alarm. In the Wales of the eighteen sixties the leadership of the denominations, which still exerted what could almost be described as a spiritual dictatorship over the lives of the majority of the Welsh people, was securely in the hands of men dedicated to many of the ideals of Thomas Arnold of Rugby. (There is indeed an interesting parallel between the father-son relationship of Lewis Edwards, the Pope of Bala, and Thomas Charles Edwards, who became the first Principal of the University of Wales, and the relationship between Thomas and Matthew Arnold.) Nationalistic sentiments and separatist aspirations were safely channelled into such unrealistic ventures as a Welsh State in Winsconsin, or Patagonia. Already the Welsh were faced with an embarrassment of choice. They could be assimilated in one way in North America, in another way in South America and in a variety of ways within the Empire. The one option that seemed not available was to go on being themselves.

The institutions of Wales, such as they were, presented no threat to the integrity of anybody except the Welsh. The Eisteddfod, which Sir John Rhys was able to describe at the end of the century as 'a thoroughly popular assembly representing the rank and file of the Welsh people . . . and a rallying point of Welshmen who live apart from one another, whether in Wales or other parts of the United Kingdom' was already securely under the control of respectable bourgeoisie anglophile social engineers like Hugh Owen. To quote Sir John Rhys again: '. . . about the middle of the present century, it struck some of the

leading Welshmen of the time that the Eisteddfod was to a considerable extent a neglected force that might be utilised for the
benefit of Wales. So Sir Hugh Owen and his friends undertook
the attempt to regulate it and to add to its meetings opportuni-
ties for discussing social and economic questions connected with
the future of Wales'.

The key verbs in this passage are *utilise* and *regulate*. They re-
veal the motives behind Hugh Owen's tireless activities.
Schools, colleges, societies, eisteddfodau, the Cymrodorion and
the network of denominational interest were all 'appliances';
active agencies for the dissemination of a comprehensive concept of social progress that he and his kind were adapting to suit
the Welsh nonconformist temperament. The chapel, that key
institution which had been brought into existence for the salvation of Welsh souls and therefore for the unspoken affirmation
of Welsh identity, could now be utilised to introduce a system
whereby the children of the most respectable and the most hard
working could be set on the road to an improved material
position in an ever improving material world. This was the moment when 'getting on' became part of the Welsh way of life.
In that eisteddfodic hierarchy of morals debased into mottoes,
'eled ymlaen' and 'dyrchafiad arall i Gymro' superseded 'y
gwir yn erbyn y byd' and 'oes y byd i'r iaith Gymraeg'. The
eisteddfod was also 'useful' to foster the competitive spirit. As
theological passions waned, social progress quietly overtook the
progress of the soul.

Arnold, in his first lecture, pokes mild fun at Hugh Owen's
eisteddfod.

> The recitation of the prize compositions began: pieces of verse and
> prose in the Welsh language, an essay on punctuality being, if I re-
> member right, one of them; a poem on the march of Havelock, an-
> other. This went on for some time.

The subjects are of course characteristic of the twin passions
of the mid-nineteenth century in Britain—utilitarianism and
imperial expansion. No doubt the subjects were set, as I believe
they still are, to please the committees and gain the approval of
the men in charge. It would not be unfair therefore to attribute
to men like Hugh Owen the noticeable coarsening of sensibility
that overtook so much of Welsh literature in the second half of

the nineteenth century. There is something peculiarly sad in the spectacle of the greatest poet of the time, Islwyn, being a consistent eisteddfodic failure. And it is ironic too that his greatest work *Y Storm* would have been the one composition of that time in the Welsh language that would have gained Matthew Arnold's enthusiastic approval. His youthful admiration for *Stürm und Drang* and the great Goethe would have helped him to recognise an affinity that escaped Welsh critics until Mr. Saunders Lewis drew attention to it in the 1950s. Alas! as far as contemporary Welsh literature was concerned Arnold, in spite of his perceptive appreciation of Lady Charlotte Guest's translation of *Y Mabinogion*, was as insensitive as any Benthamite philistine.

> . . . if an Eisteddfod author has anything to say about punctuality or about the march of Havelock, he had much better say it in English; or rather, perhaps what he has to say on these subjects may as well be said in Welsh, but the moment he has anything of real importance to say, anything the world will the least care to hear, he must speak English.

When Arnold's lectures on Celtic literature were first published in the *Cornhill Magazine*, Hugh Owen, apparently overwhelmed with admiration, and with a servility that still nauseates the reader, hastened to invite the great man to use the Chester Eisteddfod as a platform on which to read a paper on some fresh aspect of the Celtic genius. One cannot believe that such a thorough going utilitarian was so much taken with the idea of Celtic magic. 'Celtic' as a category that bundled the Welsh Calvinistic Methodists into the same bag as the Catholic Irish or Bretons or even the Wesleyan Cornish would not automatically commend itself: neither was 'magic' a word commonly used in the administration of the Poor Law or the deliberations of any of Hugh Owen's innumerable committees. What clearly delighted Owen and his friends was the prospect of doors of acceptance opening. A little more effort and a little more regulation and fresh paths of promotion and preferment would become available. Knighthoods were in sight; even O.B.E's for all. The Welsh-speaking Welsh were ideal material for the appliances of Benthamite brain washing: a proud and ancient people not actually in chains but with all their natural ambition still repressed, rendered docile by the even more effective fetters of an exacting and puritanical religion. If the price of the earthly paradise was no more than curtailing the growth of the native language this was a negligible price to pay.

It should therefore come as no surprise that when Hugh Owen's University of Wales eventually opens its doors in 1872, the national language should be overlooked. Hegel was in comfortable residence sometime before Taliesin came knocking at the door. In this kind of University, lip service was the last thing the language could expect. The first Principal, Thomas Charles Edwards was a noted preacher among the Welsh Calvinistic Methodists. He was in American political parlance 'their favourite son'. Possibly to placate some die-hards of this powerful religious constituency, and to improve the collection of quarrymen's pence, a place was found for Welsh literally in a cupboard under the stairs. (Long before Arnold's prestigious lectures, Lewis Edwards of Bala was writing to his son Thomas Charles urging him to avoid preaching in Welsh in order to improve his English style, this in spite of the fact that he himself was a Welsh writer of some distinction and editor of the best quarterly of the time *Y Traethodydd*, a magazine which I am happy to say still flourishes in spite of the forecasts of Matthew Arnold and the steady gnashing of the teeth of Hugh Owen's appliances.)

In the Welsh wonderland, this unlikely brew 'Celtic Magic' became the elixir of Assimilation. In less than a generation the University of Wales could take a Welsh Calvinistic Methodist or a Welsh Baptist and transform him with an efficiency bordering on the Japanese into an extraordinarily life-like imitation of one of Matthew Arnold's new Englishmen 'more intelligent, more gracious and more humane'. Being Welsh, which for their forefathers was compulsory, became optional for the educated, less essential than going to chapel. (This was the age of the *Inglis Côs*.) When the new Welshman stared at the Tree of Knowledge he saw two instead of one. The most dangerous thing about 'Celtic Magic' was not that it made people larger or smaller, but that it introduced a permanent state of double vision.

It must be added that 'Celtic Magic' also filled a vacuum in that vital process of myth-making whereby the tribes and the nations reaffirm their faith in their own continuing existence. History like everything else is written from a point of view. In the nation-making process it is a vital industry. In the Welsh context the historian inherits the function of the bards and the poetic tradition. The breakdown of the bardic tradition may well be interpreted as the dissolution of a nation. When it is re-placed eventually by an education system which is an amalgam of Utilitarianism and Cultural Imperialism, strange results were bound to occur. And indeed they did. And still do.

But it was in the political rather than in the poetical arena that Celtic Magic really made itself felt. Historical truth obliges us to record that without the help of any imported brew or magic bottle, for three centuries Welsh Utopias rose and fell with monotonous regularity: The Quaker Welsh Tract in the Peaceable Kingdom; Morgan John Rhys's Beulah; Robert Owen's New Harmony; Richard Lloyd-Jones's Valley of the God Almighty Jones; S.R.'s crazy Tennessee experiment (only nine miles from Thomas Hughes's Anglican Fool's Paradise, Rugby Tennessee); William Bebb's Venedotia and last but not least Michael D. Jones's Patagonia. Michael D. Jones may have failed in Patagonia but Emrys ap Iwan was surely right to describe him as the Welshman most worthy of honour. Cer-tainly his national spirit and spirited nationalism gave two young politicians that confidence in themselves and in a vision of their own kind that seems essential for the completion of a successful enterprise. Thomas E. Ellis of Cynlas farm Bala be-came a successful Liberal politician. On the way he also went to Aberystwyth University and took his first taste of 'Celtic Magic'. In a grandiose essay entitled *The Influence of the Celt in the Making of Britain*, he begins:

> I desire at the outset to express my gratitude as a student and as a Celt to Mr. Matthew Arnold and the band of literary and scientific men who determined to see things as they really are, have endeav-oured to understand the Celtic peoples and appreciate the Celtic genius.

The essay continues as a bare-faced takeover bid of all the virtues ever displayed by the peoples of Britain. Arnold's magic brew has touched off a more ancient intoxicant. Whose voice are we listening to? Taliesin's Urien Rheged or this product of Aberystwyth and Oxford?

> Is it not this very Celticism which gives to Britain that special power and genius, that distinctive gift which differentiates Britain from Germany and which gives it the pre-eminence?

Michael D. Jones's other disciple was the first Welshman to invite a Fenian to address a Welsh radical meeting. Michael Davitt and David Lloyd George appeared on the same platform at Ffestiniog in 1886. Could Arnold have been right after all to suspect that a radical and Fenian spirit was lurking in the remoter recesses of the native language? Lloyd George was aggressively Welsh and he was not encumbered with a University of Wales education. His cultural interests may have been sporadic but there was no doubt that he had *Style* in abundance, and enough Titanism to set any British audience jumping off their seats. But again Matthew Arnold's ghost can rest in peace. The most demonic personal nationalism since Iolo Morganwg's was soon harnessed to the imperial cause. In the Great War the cloak of Arthur and the white hair of Merlin were visible attributes of the Celtic Magic that led the steadfast patriotism of the English and the imperial fantasies of the peripheral Celts to victory.

It is not too crude a simplification to maintain that the Institutions of Wales, old and new, were prepared to abandon the mother tongue in exchange for a mess of pottage with Celtic Magic. But Wonderland is a country provided with a variety of antidotes. As in any other children's story, a rescue can arrive at any moment and from the most unexpected quarter. Thanks to Arnold's bare-footed sojourn on the sacred earth of Pen-y-Gogarth, a Chair of Celtic was created at Oxford. From this dizzy cultural elevation, it was inevitable in the course of time that scholarly privilege would percolate to the provincial extremities. Even at Aberystwyth, Welsh (if not Cymraeg) could come out of the cupboard under the stairs. The disciples of Sir John Rhys arrived like missionaries in the bush, burning to spread the new light of philology among their unenlightened kith and kin. But the language of instruction remained English, as Matthew Arnold would have maintained, the only appropriate medium for scientific investigation and all modern purposes.

Wonderlands are unstable. They are always liable to disappear. Someone has to sit on with closed eyes and re-create the dream, otherwise it will dissolve and be forgotten for ever. Out of Hugh Owen's Aberystwyth and into Arnold's Oxford, Owen M. Edwards came. He re-occupied that cave on Mount Helicon that had been left vacant far too long.

> Mae'r oll yn gysegredig. It is all sacred. Every hill and every valley. Our land is a living thing, not a grave of forgetfulness under our feet. Every hill has its history, every locality its own romance, every part of the landscape wears its own particular glory. And to a Welshman, no other country can be like this. A Welshman feels that the struggles of his forefathers have sanctified every field, and the genius of his people has transformed every mountain into hallowed ground. And it is feeling like this that will make him a true citizen.

Owen M. Edwards laid the foundation for a brilliant literary revival because he re-established the links between the Welsh people and their own past and made a new beginning possible. Like Matthew Arnold he made his appeal to a landscape. The difference was that he belonged to it.

The loss of incantation

'To utter a word', said Ludwig Wittgenstein, and I hope I quote him correctly, 'is to strike a note on the keyboard of the imagination'. The proposition reverberates: both as a sound and as an idea. To utter a word is to disturb the universe. It is a distinct power. The grasshopper when he rubs his legs together, the bullock breathing into the hay, the magpie cleaning his feathers, make musical contributions to a breathing planet if not to the music of the spheres: but words are of a higher order of sound, beautiful and dangerous.

Let us be arrogant and say it: words, individual words, are more wonderful than individual musical sounds. A word in silence is as inexplicable as a single footprint in a waste of snow: one note from an instrument, hand made or electronic, can cause alarm like the cry of an owl in a dark tree, or a baby in a wet cot; but in itself it does not contain its private store of in- cantation and magic.

Take as a random example the word 'Handschuh': to an English-hearing ear (which is a more logical term than an English-speaking ear) it can evoke a fleeting image of a merry Bavarian peasant dancing with his hands in his clogs and his white feet waving in the air; until linguistic training clamps down on the bounding imagination and points it towards the image of a glove. I do not wish to imply disapproval of linguistic training or suggest that it cramps the freedom of the creative imagination. It is a necessary discipline that has to be endured before we can be rewarded with a proper appreciation of such lines as

> Da fällt von des Altans Rand
> Ein Handschuh von schöner Hand . . .

whether these words be sung or spoken.

In the world of words, the genie of the imagination needs must live inside the lamp of reason. Take that charming song 'Deryn y Bwn o'r Banna'. I cannot tell what the untutored English- hearing ear would make of the words: but as a half-educated Welsh child, I always thought the title was 'Deryn y Bwn o'r Bala' and I imagined a great moulting methodist of a bird (Calvinistic not Wesleyan) with a burden strapped to its back flapping distractedly in a vain attempt to become airborne. It was only after many years of haphazard educational processing

103

that I discovered that 'aderyn y bwn' was in fact a member of the heron family and favoured the Beacons for topographical rather than theological reasons.

Words allow a writer to dress out his more nebulous hunches (there's a strange word for you) into seemingly respectable theories. I now proceed to do just this. English is a word system which has sold a large part of its power of incantation for another kind of power; a Jacob among the tongues of the earth, swopping an invisible birthright for the largest mass of pottage in the world.

We Welsh are urged to perfect our knowledge of the language of commerce; but the main poetic outlet of the language of commerce is advertising. Advertising is poetry designed for the consumption of the maximum number of units of a given market. The limits of the market are drawn by the limits of knowing the language. Words are selected to persuade every human within these limits to become a unit of consumption. Persuasion is all. Good advertisements are poetic formulae that use all the blandishments of the art with a considerable degree of success. Since he is in no way inhibited by considerations of truth and accuracy and since his interest in his audience goes no deeper than their pockets, the advertiser's hand and mind are alive with disingenuous cunning. Not only imagination but also science and technology are his obedient slaves. The extent of pockets and packets can be weighed and measured: the behaviour of masses can be analysed and predicted by eager and intelligent academic economists and psychologists. The advertiser-poet assembles a mass of information before he bursts into mellifluous song.

All these activities put a strain on the language and press it down into smooth categories of jargon that can be sliced up with scientific precision like dead flesh in gelatine. The advertiser's song is sweet with the smell of death in the funeral parlour of a language. His mode, in the musical sense, corrupts all forms of communication inside the language limits. Presentation is all, whether you are trying to sell talcum powder or a Prime Minister or a new political policy. In gaining a whole new world of affluence and power, metropolitan English has come as near as a language can to losing its own soul.

It could be argued that English lost touch with Incantation

104

around the year 1922, when the new communication systems began to tighten their grip on the mind of western man. It must be significant that one of the last sustained pieces of prosodic incantation in English poetry was written just before this date by an American who fled to Europe to escape what he took to be the tidal wave of all-conquering American-English commercial communication. The one thing a communication system cannot do is incant: and the English language is now more securely trapped inside these systems than that great prince who languished in a dark prison or the man in the iron mask.

Incantation is more than just a musical noise. I would not presume a definition: but I know it is to do with the invocation of those powers which used to be called supernatural. The fact that our civilisation has shunted off the supernatural into the anthropological section of the science museum along with boomerangs and steam locomotives, in no way diminishes the inherent urge in all sustained poetic expression to invoke and incant. When Homer, Vergil, Dante or even Milton called on the God to aid them in their massive enterprises they were not merely going through the motions of a prescribed convention. They knew they needed help: and they also knew that help had to come from outside themselves. Like David singing a psalm, or the Red Indian Shaman chanting to the Great Spirit, they knew very well that they were performing under the eye of Truth: only if they worked with respect for their material and a reverence for the world outside them had they any hope of gaining that Visitation, which would elevate their efforts to the level we still chose to call immortal. Even Berthold Brecht, that most anti-metaphysical of great poets, showed surprising reverence and humility when he sang at his best. He was happy to sing in praise of the Black Forest or such engaging bodies as the Danish-Worker-Actors or even the annual conference of the electricians union: there is no record that he ever wrote an ode in praise of Joseph Stalin.

The advertiser-poet of the communication systems is strangely confined to a narrow version of the lyric form: he is condemned to search out variations on the continuous theme of wooing a mythical average consumer. This is more difficult than writing love songs to a window-dresser's dummy. No one should presume to underrate their skill. It is a craft sufficiently versatile to

105

fill Sunday papers week after week from one end of the world to the other, dominating every page including the editorials and the photographs. Maintaining the flow of eyecatching paper-thin superficiality is far more difficult than counting how many angels can stand on the head of a pin: the superficiality is scientifically necessary. In the poetry of advertising it would be fatal failure if the satisfaction took to residing in the words themselves. *Walk tall. Drink Milwaukee Beer*: the artificer would be distressed, and soon unemployed, if his object of his affection, the willing consumer, walked *away* from the tempting tavern, contentedly mulling over the immortal phrase. *Black Magic* is meant to be eaten, not spoken. In the cannibalism of advertising, the victims are words.

In our civilisation incantation has been diminished to the weaving of spells and this function has been completely transferred from language to scientific technology. A Boeing 747 is more effective than a magic carpet not merely because it can actually transfer a slab of trusting humanity from one continent to another at clock-confusing speed; it can also speak. It has a menacing roar that can madden men and burn up more air than would be needed by a million aeolean harps. It is an object of worship. The workers of a city can devote their entire working hours to its creation. A national economy can bankrupt itself trying to build a more massive rival. It can transport three or four symphony orchestras from one metropolis to another: this can seem strangely impressive in itself, worthy of an enthusiastic newspaper article about international standards and a laudatory television actuality film: but in fact these talented men are no more than budgerigars shuttled about in the more gilded channels of the commerce of machines. The music that matters is made by internal combustion engines, box-office tills, the food mixers used by musicians' wives, the air-conditioner, the dishwashing machine, the waste disposal unit.

Our advanced civilisation provides us with affluence and comfort on a scale previously reserved for princes. The loss of incantation in poetry and music may be thought a small price to pay, as we stagger out of the supermarket laden with goodies for every member of the family. The music of the machines may be a bit nerve-wracking: but Daddy can always lock himself up in his sound-proof study and refresh his jaded sensibilities with a superb recording of a Beethoven quartet on his new stereo. After all, he was brought up in the old school and conditioned to enjoy the preserved fruits of the old high-bourgeois European culture. Upstairs, above the generation gap, a younger and more eager audience is listening to more raucous sounds that are the product of the contemporary American experience: the agonised cries of young sacrificial figures. Our civilisation, which is dedicated to providing a unit of heaven to every satisfactory citizen, needs a thin but steady trickle of sacrificial figures, inspired sufferers who will provide broken liturgical noises and safety valve litanies that will help to give the whole system the old human flavouring.

It was not by chance that young Robert Vimmermann changed his name to Bob Dylan. In the computerised filing systems that help to maintain our consensus of well-being, poets and prophets are found under the same code, all proxy-suffering, out-dropping, colourful, idiosyncratic, long-haired non-conformists scheduled to be briefly indulged but ultimately doomed. The change of name was in itself an act of incantation. The mantle of a prophet and the singing robes of a poet were packed in the parachute of a single Welsh name. And the incantation succeeded. One human native was temporarily transformed and the music of transformation disturbed the surface calm of a new generation like a sudden breeze on an expanse of leaden water. The effect was not lasting. In our system the poet-prophet-musician is obliged like Attis and Dionysius to die young. If he is not killed off by an aeroplane crash or war he is doomed to drown in alcohol or wealth and leave his image behind like a sacramental wafer for yet another splinter cult.

It appears that the massive thrust of commercial technology is imposing a new uniform culture over the entire world. Factory plants, airports, assembly lines, oil tankers require identical facilities wherever they appear and they bring with them a way of life which is the same whether you find yourself in Tacoma or Tonypandy, Amlwch or Aarhus or Arizona. Differences of race, climate, language, culture are buried alive under the new superstructure. In no time at all communication systems are re-modelled to meet the needs of this new superstructure. In a matter of a generation tribes and nations are forced to adapt themselves to the new conditions, and culture shifts take place

on a scale that can only be compared to those awe-inspiring sub-
terranean movements that cause earthquakes. Like earthquakes, culture shifts make people feel tiny and helpless and
ready to rush into the nearest available shelter, sobbing and
breathless with gratitude; or blind with anger and impotent
rage.

In the United States a great pattern of cracks and wrinkles in
the cooling racial and cultural melting pot has been covered
with extraordinary speed by a smooth layer of English-speaking
commercial technology: a vast white continental wedding cake
decorated with campuses and concert halls. This vigorous and
generous society spends more on decorating a bigger cake than
any of its European cousins: nevertheless, the true pulse of its
poetry still comes through the persuasion media. Poets, actors,
singers, rush into the communications arena with the astonish-
ing energy and aggression of gladiators in a rodeo: they expend
their talents with frenetic generosity to satisfy a public appetite
that is the more insatiable for not being easily assuaged by pre-
cooked poetry substitutes.

Underneath all this, the smaller European cultures, subsist,
becoming more and more like Indian 'nations' on Reservations: increasingly inclined to gear their cultural effort for small
handcraft export or tourist entertainment. On the one hand, an
eisteddfod can be made international and catch cream and
crumbs from the tourist table; on the other hand, universities
can plug into the superstructure by capturing large grants from
councils, corporations, oil companies or government agencies,
and use the sterilised lucre as manna for the maintenance of
high standards, excellence of performances, and bigger and
better synthesisers. Since we are all beneficiaries of the great
superstructure, we all tend towards an uncritical helplessness
that suggests it would be the height of bad manners to be caught
trying to bite the hand that feeds us. There are, after all, artists
who sing and celebrate the beauties of the new superstructure:
for example, Rodgers and Hammerstein. Their relationship to
the great American dream is exactly analogous to the function
of Mozart and da Ponte in their aristocratic society. It could be
argued that the musical product has to be watered down and
sugared up to cater for the massive increase in the size of the
audience. But the process of vulgarisation (in the strictest sense)

has to take place unconsciously: no one can create with his tongue wedged hard into his cheek. An artist is obliged to respect his audience as much as his material. He must have humility as well as self-assurance. It is consoling to remember that Bach never worried about the international market. He catered for the needs of a particular audience who shared his language, his beliefs, his preconceptions, his attitudes. An artist who incants always performs a public function. He depends on his public. He emerges from his audience as a blossom grows from the branch of a tree. The blossom and the tree are joined together in an organic unity of purpose and function that has evolved over a long period of time. In the European tradition the tree is the language and the long literary tradition that belongs to it.

We are all aware that the lines of communication in the technological superstructure are controlled by mysterious powers that appear to be as remote and as divine as the God of the Old Testament. Like the ancient Hebrews, different academic disciplines indicate the nature of this power with different respectful synonyms. Whatever it is, it is self-existent: and whether the outward economic and political forms are capitalist or communist, the superstructure, like any sophisticated machine, exists to perpetuate the rare perfection of its own functioning. It does not need to be sustained by any sound of incantation other than its own working noise. Fundamentally, the incantatory poet and musician are socially redundant. The superstructure does not need them. It can use them and make use of them: but 'crying need' is not there. The Indian at the wheel of his Cadillac or the Welsh professor on Sabbatical leave may have patronising thoughts about their ululating ancestors: they may persuade themselves they have inherited the full extent of the earthly paradise right up to the doors of the crematorium. The poet, alas, is not permitted these easy forms of self-assurance or release. He still has to concern himself with the tattered concept of eternity, and unscientific discredited eternal verities. This can be tough. Witness a Soviet writer under house arrest, any campus poet drowning his impotence in gin or an old reservation Indian singing to the setting sun in a language he is the very last to use. Somehow in his own weak person if he can the poet must reconcile the glories of the tribal past with the grim exigencies of the tribal present, and do this within the stern discipline of the tribal language.

The tribal language, be it Welsh, Danish, Dutch, Magyar or Greek may have many disabilities, but it is reasonably safe to assume that it is several degrees less demythologised than the major languages of the communication systems. Bartok's music. Pantycelyn's words, Kirkegaard's sermons, Seferis' poems are all saturated with the power of incantation. But this power did not come from isolated individuals: they spoke with a gift of tongues which they inherited from their tribe. A poet like Robert Williams Parry can make numinous a poem about a fox or a weasel so that his disciplined poetic art becomes a celebration of human existence and its extraordinary and mysterious relationship to the breath-catching beauty of a world which is part of a universe extrapolated to eternity: but he does it with the accumulated skill of generations of poets in a language which has weathered the storms of centuries.

In Wales we know from tribal experience, which is the only indispensable knowledge, that a threatened language can also be a life-line that ties in firmly to a human past. The individual talent is never alone and its efforts, however meagrely rewarded in material terms, are more life-enhancing than painting false cherries on an advertizer's cake. Precisely because he is shackled by a language steeped in tradition and honour, precisely because he is denied the freedom to be totally exploited by the mechanical universe of a communication system, he is given the opportunity to enlarge and extend the tribal experience and work with 'the uncreated consciousness of his race'.

It may be that musicians may claim to create new sounds with new electronic devices. But they cannot create a new language in the antiseptic solitude of the laboratory. Sounds just as much as words need organic growth and structure: they must in some sort communicate. If it is true that all the main channels of communication in our system are preempted by the 'power without a name' then the musician is not exempt from the dilemma of the poet. At one moment or another in his history he should find himself under some form of house arrest: or at least addressing a lonely incantation to the setting sun outside an empty tent. And he should not shrink from the experience. The keyboard of the imagination is a delicate instrument: it is also astonishingly tough.

Television and us:
reflections on a
troubled relationship

We may as well begin this discussion by accepting the given fact that the 'picture' has become the central factor of the process of communication in our time. This in itself is a disturbing challenge to a nation whose continued existence has depended on a tradition which gives pride of place to the 'word', whether spoken or written. Such culture struggles as have troubled the quiet water of Wales up to the modern age were largely conflicts between the oral and the literary: before these had been satisfactorily solved, the new technology has overtaken us and presented us with what appears to be a cultural life and death situation.

It might be helpful to begin a definition of the word 'picture' in this context. The most relevant way would be to trace the spiritual pedigree and the material development of the mechanised picture we call a photograph. This common object does boast a very high pedigree indeed: nothing less than the attempts of the great minds of the European Renaissance to plumb the depths of the meaning of existence. We might consider the work of such a versatile genius as Albrecht Dürer. Dürer was the son of a goldsmith of Magyar extraction. He was trained in his father's workshop to engrave pictures on metal surfaces. This was the age of da Vinci, Michaelangelo, Bellini, but it was Dürer more than anyone else who perfected the techniques of engraving prepared plates for reproductive printing on paper. This technique was the basis of his fame and his wealth. But Dürer was a product of the Renaissance and he thought of himself not only as an artist and as a practising capitalist, but also as a philosopher and a natural scientist. For him the German word *kunst* meant both the skill to create and produce and a philosophic understanding of these activities so that throughout his life whatever developments he made he would be inclined to justify in scientific discourse. Like Leonardo he was always conscious of the significance of any technical development for which he had been responsible. Thus, the development of perspective had more far reaching consequences than mere alteration in painting style. The development of perspective—'The technique of representing a

113

solid substance on a smooth surface in order to create an identical impression of relationships, size and distance as that which is given by the object itself when looked at from a given viewpoint'—was nothing less than evidence of the new vision gained by Renaissance Man, a vision which included the meaning of human existence, the relationship between man in society, in his environment and in the universe. The technique of perspective or some elements of it were not unknown in the classical world. But it was the artists of the Renaissance who saw its possibilities as a new basis for art and as a regular, even scientific method for imitating nature. It is worthwhile bearing in mind that perspective does not play a part of any importance in the art of non-European cultures. Even in Europe it meant nothing in the Middle Ages. We are obliged to accept that perspective, like capitalism, experimental science and industrial development, is a product of an eruption of the human spirit that we find convenient to refer to as the Renaissance and the Reformation. Furthermore it is no accident that Dürer, like Cranach and other German artists, were staunch followers and admirers of Martin Luther, and that along with their *kunst* went the first sign of a new and more acute national consciousness. For other historical reasons a variety of this consciousness already existed in Wales.

A proper treatment of this theme would need to dwell in detail on the development of artistic and scientific techniques in Europe. As it is one must leap over three centuries to concentrate on the feat of *Nicephore Niepce*. In the year 1826 he succeeded in producing the first authentic photograph by the reaction of sunlight on a prepared metal surface. Niepce was a scientist, but his more famous collaborator Daguerre was a man of the theatre, a professional stage designer. It was Daguerre who went on to perfect his discovery and turn it into a commercial proposition. But it was the intention of both men to extend the limits of artistic representation and in particular the lithographic and print methods that had formed such an important part of Albrecht Dürer's commercial success three centuries earlier. To their joy, and indeed to everyone else's, the camera lens saw the world from a viewpoint of perfect perspective. In keeping with the spirit of the age the photograph seemed to accentuate the comforting solidity of the material

114

world, and gave to it a new form of immortality on paper. The *camera obscura* was more than a toy: it was a magical machine for the mass production of votive objects for a new found materialistic faith. In the early years it was quite an expensive process. Only the rich could afford to possess a Daguerrotype. For a short time they were more fashionable than paintings; but by the middle of the nineteenth century rapid technical developments brought photography within the reach of any family of reasonable means. Its size and reproduction became a recognised symbol of success in every sphere of modern life. W. E. Gladstone, Louis Napoleon, Bismark, glowered down from the wallpaper of the homes of all their loyal subjects in the new nation states that dominated European life. Artists like Charles Dickens and Henrik Ibsen, delighted in giving their young female admirers signed photographs of themselves; and even the French Impressionists, when driven by poverty, would use landscape photographs to remind them of the joys of the places they could not afford to visit. It is only in this century that photography was appreciated as something more than an extension of painting and developed from being a social toy into an essential item of equipment in all aspects of scientific research. Such developments inevitably reinforced the strength of its position in the social anthropology of the modern world. Here was the ready made iconography of a new world religion.

It is pertinent to attempt an enumeration of some of the more obvious characteristics of the photograph. From the economic point of view it has provided the capitalists with a product that can be reproduced to a point of theoretical infinity. We may think for example of taking the perfèct colour photograph of Cwm Pennant and then reproducing it on the spot until the valley itself is obliterated and the Drws y Coed mountain gradually sinks out of sight. By the same token the photograph of a parliamentary candidate could be sufficiently reproduced to obliterate the constituency he seeks to represent. These are considerations we shall return to later on in the agrument. What needs to be claimed at this point is that the photograph is the most effective and exact record of the surface of life on earth that man has ever invented. If this were only half true then the concept of History as an academic discipline with some claim to scientific method, has been utterly changed for ever. It is possible that few documentary accounts of events will stand comparison with the photograph and its terrible offspring the film in the significance of the factual information that they will provide. A photograph can literally 'speak volumes' about the nature of a building, a machine, a landscape, a man and the civilisation which sustains him in unparalleled material comfort. Furthermore the photograph has revealed aspects of life that were never previously visible. Ultra-violet and Infra-red have added as much to the power of the human eye as the motor car has extended the power of the human foot: and it is such extensions to the human capacity for communication that have put all language into question. As a lingua franca, as a means of social regulation and instruction, photography and its attendant rituals seem to have progressed well beyond the range of the Latin of the mediaeval world.

iii

Part of the strength of the new language must be its exceptionally simple grammar and syntax. Because it has no words it appears to be untrammelled by the fiddling details that go with verbs and sentences and none of the obsolete sophistication of initial consonant mutation. It is built for speed of execution and instant registration. It is excessively democratic. A photograph is capable of draping the most trivial moment with monumental importance and elevating the least significant object to immortal status. With or without the skill of a photographer there is little to choose between a snapshot of a royal wedding or a well lit picture of a piece of orange peel in the gutter. Whatever our allegiance, we have to accept that the photograph detaches an object or its subject from its physical place in the order of nature and from our experience of it in the course of animated living. It has a dangerous detachment. The man who pays the cameraman has an infinite variety of pliant picture material available for manipulation.

An individual still picture can have its own alarming intimations of eternity. Because of its apparent removal from the world of space and time, of growth and decay, of birth and life, the frozen moment lasts for ever. Take as example a famous picture of Ypres in 1917. It can be dwelt upon for ever and represent a universe torn apart and extending from the nothing

116

inside itself to a mirror fixed in another galaxy. Or a photograph taken in Biafra or Kampuchia: heaps of skulls in a clearing in a forest, the bodies of starved children. No cruelty is ever to be forgotten or forgiven.

We come now to a paradox in the nature of the photograph. Its surface appears to be excessively and often unbearably real. And yet in its essence it is an illusion designed to create the impression of a presence. An illustrated cookery book presents mouth-watering images of meals that can hardly be equalled in reality. Every successful publisher in this field knows that he must delude the ambitious queen of the kitchen in exactly the same way as Gwydion succeeded in deluding Pryderi. For a portfolio of photographs of thoroughbreds he obtained a herd of genuine pigs. An illusion, of course, can turn to magic not only in the Mabinogion but also throughout the entire world from the moment when the technical descendants of Durer and Daguerre succeeded in creating the impression that the photograph could move. This is not the place to dwell on the development of moving pictures that began in France and America in the 1890's and created a form of industrial culture which fulfilled with scientific precision the leisure needs of the industrial masses throughout the developed world. But it is necessary to note a vital element essential both to the production and the display of films. Every individual frame has to remain still in the light for its appropriate fraction of a second in order to create the impression of movement. That is to say in the mechanical reality of both the camera and the projector the still moves and the movement is stillness. This is the reality behind the magic, the trick at the heart of the illusion. And it is more than a willing suspension of disbelief. The great cosmos of the cinema, like any other false religion, has been built up on an universally acceptable deception.

iv

It was no accident that the most thriving centre of this new industry of dreams and illusions should be established on the far West shore of the United States of America. There remains an intimate psychological and physiological connection between the Californian El Dorado and the dream factories of Hollywood. Since the Renaissance and the discovery of the New

World the classical dreams of Arcadia and the earthly Paradise were transferred from the Mediterranean to the new continent beyond the ocean that once poured over the edge of the known world. By the end of the nineteenth century the greatest migration in the history of the world had taken place. Millions of workers and peasants from all over Europe poured into the new continent, some fleeing from famine but all in search of a dream. Instead of the distant Paradise they found the back streets of New York, Detroit, Chicago, and entered a spiritual captivity in a concrete Babylon. For children lost in the forest of cities what better diversion than sitting in the dark auditorium to watch the wordless antics of Charlie Chaplin, a brave little man facing obstacles so like the ones they faced but unlike them always able to overcome them. Like the illusion itself flickering on the screen he was preserved by magical means and they gained temporary relief from their tribulations by laughing at him. Like the photograph the cinema could speak without words and entertain everyone whatever their language or their circumstances. By 1914 this new art form, the first to grow out of industrial technology had become firmly rooted in the hearts of the common people throughout the United States and the most remarkable aspect of this conquest was the way in which it reached the innermost parts of their minds and hearts without ever having to knock at the front door of a spoken language. It entered with the stealth of a thief in the night and took possession of a new empire.

While Chaplin was cheering up the spiritual refugees in far away America, the first World War erupted in Europe to throw mountains of rubble between us and traditional European culture. In less than three years Lenin had journeyed through Germany in his sealed train to lead the Russian Revolution. By the end of that war the pattern of the modern world, our world, had begun to emerge and nothing illustrates our condition more clearly than the development of film both as an art form and as an industry. Whoever controlled this new world would also need to control the machinery of magic and illusion. What was the fate of the cinema to be? Would it continue to feed the fantasies of a deracinated proletariat in order to make great fortunes for sleazy capitalists? Or would it serve the socialist revolution and help to create a new order, an authentic materialist, socialist paradise on earth? Throughout the revolution, the Russian film industry enjoyed the favour, indeed the firm embrace of the authority of the Bolshevist government. Lenin declared that film was the most important form of culture. It could be moulded as the most effective medium to instruct and control the people in the task of creating a new Communist society. It was the only way to make contact with all nationalities in a revolutionary period, to carry the vital message across the boundaries of language, to lead all the peoples along the peaceful paths of propaganda to the promised land.

For sixty years film production has reflected with great accuracy the polarisation of the political world. On the Western extremity the capitalist resources of the United States built cardboard castles for the mass production of dreams to respond to the emancipated appetite, to kindle the imagination and tap the pocket of every would-be playboy of the Western world. Photographs of desirable individuals in enviable situations were reproduced and distributed in uniform units like packets of chocolate or shredded wheat for regular consumption. Like the star system the basic principle was established early and continues to operate on even more sophisticated levels in the television industry. The picture is the icon of the cult of personality. In the socialist East dreams needed to be more realistic. To be effective propaganda a vision must be expressed in shapes that bear a recognisable relationship to reality. During the early period, entry to the picture halls in Russia was often free of charge. Commercial advantage was never the prime object so that the picture makers could concentrate on influencing the hearts and minds of the audience. This difference of motivation was responsible for notable differences in style and technique. Across the world film makers were acutely conscious of each other's work. Eisenstein for instance was heavily under the influence of D. W. Griffiths, and was very ready to acknowledge this. But before the Stalin dictatorship, he and others were able to develop montage and make film photography a more flexible and subtle language.

The concept of polarisation must not allow us to ignore what was happening in the centre, to a Europe whose foundations of bourgeois culture were cracked by the first World War. The most significant contrast lay between the victors and the van-

119

quished. It was in Germany that a brilliant film industry developed and it was the inspiration of this industry that set the pace. On the whole the contribution of victorious England and its British Empire to this new medium was surprisingly weak and ineffective. At least part of the reason must be attributed to the absence of revolution and radical social change. Just as George V was still on his throne, the stars of the West End of London still reigned happily over an entertainment world which was designed to reflect with a minimum of change the life of the English middle class. In contrast with the intelligentsia on the Continent, the English were inclined to keep as closely as they could to their accustomed standards and interests in literature and the arts. The cinema was little better than flicks in the flea-pit and the working class, whenever it was noticed, was deemed loyal and deserving of alternating pats on the head and the back. When the industrial workers attempted to rouse themselves from their political slumber, in 1926, they were soon driven back to their lairs in the slums by the self-discipline, self-confidence and full bellies of healthy young men from public schools assisted by the classics and rules of the cricket field as well as the army and the police. England in the twenties was no place for experimenting.

v

Nevertheless the English quietly developed a mass medium that appeared to be all their very own. They were too pragmatic a people to ignore all the obvious advantages of so cheap and efficient a medium as the wireless to a central government with a great empire to administer. Quite apart from this, sound radio was without doubt more acceptable than film to the literary culture of a middle-class which was intent on running the British Empire as if nothing had changed in the world. Spoken English was the silken chain designed by Providence to bind this far-flung Empire together and the microphone was the natural instrument for its dissemination. With unusual speed and uncharacteristic enthusiasm the governing class built in the heart of London a massive temple to house the small microphone that could keep in touch with the extremities of an Empire on which the sun never set. Through the medium of this miraculous little instrument words of comfort and encouragement could reach the ears of all the faithful citizens of the King-

Emperor, from the hills of Kasha to the hills of Ceredigion. Except for the purpose of comedy, these words were always spoken in an Oxford accent of ineffable refinement. (Anyone who doubts this should take a look at a book on spoken English by a former teacher of phonetics and the honorary secretary of the B.B.C. advisory committee in that period, Professor A. Lloyd James, needless to say a Welshman. The title of the book is 'The Broadcast Word'.)

It is instructive to take a look at the architecture of Broadcasting House of which photographs are invariably taken from a low angle. What indeed is this but a battleship at anchor? And what is the figurehead but Ariel, Prospero's agent, who can now promise to encircle the world in half a second instead of forty minutes in order to prove that Britannia will go on ruling the waves of the air long after she has been obliged to relinquish her control of the waves of the sea.

The microphone, like the camera, has its own strangely contradictory attributes. By today it is particularly accessible, easy to handle, durable and very cheap to maintain. This was not the case in the early days, and the British Broadcasting Company was anxious to prevent it falling into the hands of the 'wrong people'. In Wales particularly, the Broadcasting Company was inclined to argue that the dialect of so mountainous a region could never be picked up or transmitted on so delicate an instrument, even if it could be proved that the dialect in question was worthy of such favoured treatment. The story of Welsh broadcasting in the twenties and thirties is a depressing anticipation of the grim story of television in the sixties and seventies. The interesting correlation for the purpose of this thesis lies between the physical nature of the invention, the political social and cultural problems involved in its exploitation and the consistent themes in the excuses provided by the controlling authorities in not allowing the use of the new technology in the service of the native culture.

Consider the microphone again. Even today it does not work all that well unless it is placed at the correct angle to the lips of the speaker or the source of the sound. Worse than this it has little power to differentiate between various kinds of sounds. This used to mean, and to some extent it still means, that it is almost impossible to create a perfect sound studio. It demands what is virtually a vacuum and to make a perfect recording of a given sound you have also to devise a means of keeping the speaker alive for at least as long as it necessary for him to finish what he has to say. These difficulties were easily elevated to the level of a mystique, and when the B.B.C. possessed a monopoly of sound radio it was not slow to take advantage of the fact.

Acute technical difficulties arose when talking and sound was introduced into the film industry. For a while it brought the development of a promising art form to a literal standstill. The studio floor was renamed the sound stage, the microphone became the tempramental centre of the entire operation. The best directors from Hollywood to Moscow, Chaplin, Pudovkin, Eisenstein and the rest rebelled in vain against the oppression of this tiny dictator. In film after film the key scene became the moment when the hero and his girl faced each other lovingly across a restaurant table with a convenient bunch of flowers between them concealing the microphone. The golden age of the silent screen had come to an end, and its creative period had been even shorter than the equivalent flowering of the London theatre in Elizabethan England.

vi

So industrialised an art form, whether under capitalism or socialism, would appear to give little scope to the individual talent. It is all the more consoling therefore to observe from the history of the cinema that in spite of all the restrictions, the most memorable creations bear the hallmark of individuality just as much as a poem, a novel or a play. Here again film reflects with great accuracy the paradox inherent in the human condition in the modern world. It was during the golden age of the silent cinema that one man set about creating, virtually single-handed, the form of cinema which has proved in the end to have been the most influential and to have had the greatest impact on the use of the 'picture', either still or moving, in the business of communication. Robert Flaherty was a wild romantic explorer whose early life was a sequence of proto-typical frontier journeys, often in pursuit of an earthly paradise that might also turn out to be an El Dorado. Only when the camera was in his hands was he presented with the extraordinary opportunity of translating his dream into a new form of visual reality. With what we might like to call Celtic flare or even Taliesinic inspiration, he seized on the most powerful element inherent in the nature of the photograph, namely its capacity to reproduce the surface of the visible world and the processes of living with phenomenal accuracy and documentary attention to detail. Against the prevailing torrent of Hollywood escapism this Irish American poet and dreamer created the heroic originals of the documentary film: *Nanook of the North, Moana,* and later *Man of Arran.* One need not go as far as to say that only an individualistic Irishman could have achieved this. Nevertheless there are strange historical echoes attached to his career. Like St. Brendan, his early life was a series of launches into the unknown. Later, when the moguls of Hollywood lost patience with his undisciplined poetic habits, he turned eastwards like an Irish missionary of the Dark Ages, carrying with him the secrets of his new gospel.

The turning point in his career and in the future development of the film industry in Britain occurs in Berlin in the year 1930. Flaherty had gone there in order to make direct contact with the leaders of the film industry in Russia. Pudovkin and Eisenstein were eager to co-operate with the 'Father of the Documentary Film', as Flaherty was already nicknamed, and he himself had a high regard for the work of the Russians. Berlin was still the intellectual capital for European film makers and a centre of experiment in the arts. Unfortunately for Flaherty and probably for European civilization, Stalin had decided to tighten the reins on film directors just as much as on the Soviet State in general. He was in no mood to allow freedom of experiment. The international possibilities inherent in the nature of the medium and in the genius of the men who were longing to collaborate had to be abandoned.

Flaherty was stranded in Berlin. He had no work and he had no money, and he was in low spirits. It was his wife who picked up the telephone, after seven o'clock in order to take advantage of the cheap rate, to speak to John Grierson in London. (It is as well to bear the cost of the call in mind, when we look at the latest set of figures sent flashing across our Welsh firmament by the Chairman of the Welsh Advisory Council of the B.B.C.) This turned out to be an epoch making conversation. Flaherty was invited to London to work in the film department of a new establishment with the imposing name of 'Empire Marketing

Board'. This was a crucial step in the history of the development of the New Media in Britain. It was in London, of course, that Flaherty received the necessary support to produce the seminal *Man of Arran*. Other influences were at work. Because of the international respect Flaherty had gained, the English cultural establishment was at last willing to take the documentary film seriously. The sons of well-to-do families came down from Oxford and Cambridge, fired with excitement about a new art form. This also coincided with a period of economic crisis and the spectre of fascism taking shape on the international horizon. These same young men also took to left-wing political views and the romantic English spirit found political expression in a way that it had not done since the heady days of the French Revolution and the Napoleonic Wars. John Grierson was a shrewd Scotsman and he understood how to channel all these energies and create the only tradition of lasting importance in British film making. Grierson succeeded in gaining government support for the establishment for a Crown Film Unit. A style was established which was in effect an adaptation of Flaherty's method of work. Poetry was infiltrated with propaganda. The results were of great interest, but the more important long term effect was the foundation of a way of presenting the world which remains the basis of British television style to this day.

vii

The impact of film on Welsh life in the twenties had been curiously limited. Cinemas remained dark and dubious institutions, with their screens more often than not occupied by aliens flourishing long cigarette holders and lounging on tiger skins. The chapel vestry was still a more congenial centre of entertainment. Creative tensions were still at work between the spoken and the written word, between oral and literary culture, between a profound traditional conservatism and an increasing demand for novelty. Public halls and vestrys had to be booked well in advance for a choir practice or a drama rehearsal. Local Eisteddfodau North and South seemed to flourish as much as they had ever done even in Mabon's day, and the charabanc and motor-coach greatly expanded the catchment area for competitors. Welsh Wales remained as conservative in its outlook on the nature of entertainment as did the West End of London or the Windsor of King George V. For that matter, there were still pulpit giants in operation. A John Williams Brynsiencyn, a Lewis, Tumble, or a Philip Jones, Porthcawl could attract as large an audience as the most sensational film. Welsh public figures who showed any interest in the new art form were few and far between and always very young, and usually ex-service men. Ifan ap Owen Edwards, the founder of Urdd Gobaith Cymru, was an enthusiastic amateur film maker. Cynan, still to become the impresario of a reformed Gorsedd at the national Eisteddfod, showed a lively interest. Saunders Lewis was among the few literary critics to show an early and intelligent appreciation of the medium.

During the Depression the cinema in the South Wales valley took on a new function. As Gwyn Thomas describes it, it was a refuge and a shelter for the unemployed and their children, helping them to forget their hunger. It was here more than anywhere else that the new medium was able to slip into its pre-destined social role in modern society. As in the America of the Depression, escapism became more than an escape to a people confronted with an unbearably grim reality. In 1931 the secretary of the Empire Marketing Board managed to rustle up £2,500 to make a film about industrial craftsmanship in England. After many vicissitudes Flaherty shot it with his unique poetic eye and Grierson wrote the smart progressive commentary. This was the landmark that was to open up the whole of industrial Britain as a subject for the documentary film, a development which was to include South Wales and its condition as a very suitable case for treatment.

viii

The documentary movement reached its zenith of power and influence in London during the war. Under the Ministry of Information talented directors such as Basil Wright and Humphrey Jennings were given an unusual degree of freedom and financial support to create films that would stiffen the morale of the people, lift the hearts of the masses and generally help the war effort. At a time of crisis the power of a new art form was harnessed in order to fulfil the age old function of the poet—to celebrate the existence of the tribe and stiffen its resolve to

125

triumph over difficulties and resist attack. It was only now that the flicks became respectable and ripe for inclusion as part of the English heritage. But even at the moment of triumph, the promise was never realised. After the war the London based film industry was struck by a very painful disease—elephantitis. The spirit of Empire still kindled in the hearts of capitalists like J. Arthur Rank. He was too rigidly set in the imperial mould to understand that the world had changed for ever. He could not bear to see the U.S. monopolise the world market for films with English language sound tracks. This was his language that they were daring to exploit for such mouthwatering profits. In his way he was even more romantic than Robert J. Flaherty, seeing himself like St. George riding out to do battle with the American dragon. Unfortunately he had none of Flaherty's talent and as things were, the dragon was a good deal stronger than the saint. He and his horse were swallowed up in no time. The sacrifice of the documentary film in the interests of the neo-imperial big picture had been all in vain, and its early promise had been blighted for nothing.

The forties were lean years both for the documentary film and for the young men who had been trained in the traditions of Flaherty and John Grierson. They suffered a period of unemployment and homelessness, but this did not last for long. In London even as one door closes another always opens. It was at this time that the B.B.C. decided to reopen and expand its television service. Many of the pioneers of the documentary film found a new home at Alexandra Palace, Finsbury Park. It was a new home with prospects, but in the early years of only limited comforts. To explain why this should be so we must return to the image of Ariel at the mast-head of the headquarters in Portland Place. These geographical situations are important. When the microphone was like the harp of David playing its delectable accompaniment to the verbal culture of the ruling English middle class, Finsbury Park was almost as far outside the Pale as Ferndale or Aberystwyth. The relative importance of public institutions were to be measured by the literal distance between them and the heart of the Empire at Westminster and the Royal Palace. The B.B.C. had been created as a cultural extension to the Civil Service. Like the Indian Civil Service on which it was modelled, it was staffed by men trained in the public school concept of service. The traditional qualities required were a deep respect for the classics, particularly the Romans, Cicero and Julius Caesar; self discipline and control over the emotions; an unspoken but unswerving adherence to the imperial ideal of exercising benevolent rule over the rest of humanity; an inclination to self-sacrifice or at least self-effacement in the service of a higher cause, and above all else perhaps an ability to make decisions and deliver firm and equivocal orders. The B.B.C. was created to be the last refuge of the imperial mandarin class. This was the pattern laid down by Sir John Reith and to this day heads of department in the B.B.C. are designated by initials in exactly the same way as the Civil Service. The system that spread out from the headquarters at Portland Place had many virtues: but it was not the most obvious refuge for displaced persons from the documentary film industry; neither was it sufficiently flexible to house and nourish an alternative British culture which still lingered like a forgotten garrison in the mountainous outpost known as Wales.

ix

Here literary culture had survived the Act of Union through the strenuous collaboration of men of the Renaissance and the more enlightened members of the old bardic order. When the natural leaders of society abandoned the native culture it was cherished by the lower classes and maintained in a sufficiently healthy state until the population explosion that accompanied industrialisation in the early nineteenth century made possible what was in effect a new nation. Unique among the Celtic communities on the north-west seaboard of Europe, the Welsh enjoyed a relative prosperity. They became a literate people taught by the discipline of religious nonconformity to value books and education and inspired by indigenous institutions such as the eisteddfod to attempt ambitious cultural projects, to excel in a variety of forms of self-expression and to take delight in such arts as were accessible to them. They also became politically conscious and socially ambitious and it was this last characteristic above all others that made them exceptionally vulnerable to the great changes that were taking place in British society as a whole.

127

It would not be correct to claim that the 1870 Education Act was a deliberate death sentence pssed on the indigenous peasant culture of Wales. In spite of the racist animosity towards the Welsh Language so often displayed by *The Times* in the mid-nineteenth century, we are obliged to accept that the most influential leaders of Welsh life at that time, men like Dr. Lewis Edwards, Sir Hugh Owen, and the Rev. John Griffiths, the Eisteddfod reformer, were falling over themselves in their anxiety to obtain an English education for their people. The 'Welsh Not' was not a pleasant ornament to hang around a child's neck on a Friday afternoon, but we have to remember that it was Welsh schoolmasters for the most part that perpetuated the custom. The majority of the people seemed to be eager to acquire the best that both linguistic worlds had to offer and were quite prepared to see their children suffer in such a good cause. To the faithful, Welsh could well be the language of heaven; but on this earth they only had to look around them to see that English was the language of commerce and worldly success. So long as a proper balance was maintained between the claims of church and state on their allegiance, they could see no reason why the blessings of bilingualism could not continue to shower on their irreproachable heads for ever. Indeed, such was the perfection of philosophical balance on the tightrope of their condition, that it was possible for them to think of English as a prize awarded to them by providence as a reward for conducting such virtuous lives within the confines of their native language.

Alas, the forces of history rarely operate in such an obliging fashion. From the time of that Education Act, the Welsh people were drawn into the popular cultural of England and into a veritable whirlpool of change. And they were tossed into that whirlpool in the most vulnerable condition possible. At a time when they needed it most, they were beginning to lose confidence in the strength of their own language, their own culture, and even their own institutions. (At the time when they acquired English the three volume novel had already passed the peak of its popularity and impact in England.) During the eighteen nineties at least three new media arrived on the scene to compete with each other for the affections of the populace and the right to function as the appropriate channels for mythology and popular story telling. The cheap novel became a reality and brought the concept of the best seller within reach of anyone who had learnt to read English in the new system of Elementary schools. But more important than these was the advent of the daily newspaper.

The Welsh people had newspapers of their own. About the same year as the *Daily Mail* began its mission of enlightening opinion and giving society a lead, *Trysorfa'r Plant*, the Calvinistic Methodist children's paper, had a circulation of its own of 45,000. Nothing is more remarkable in nineteenth century Wales than the output of the printing presses. Every denomination had its journals, its newspapers and magazines and the whole of Wales seemed to be covered by a remarkable distribution system. This was an achievement of the common people themselves and there were moments when the whole country seemed ripe for an unexampled flowering of literate democracy. What it came to enjoy in reality was an unholy combination of the talents of Lord Northcliffe and David Lloyd George. A newspaper is of course always more than a purveyor of news. Indeed for the most part this is the least of its functions. What it presents day in and day out is a way of looking at the world. It is a 'picture' of the world, a perspective in Dürer's sense of the word which is mythical in its essence and yet persuades the reader that reality is grounded in the comfortable relationship that exists between him as a reader and what is going on in the great wide world. Just as a prosperous burgher could buy a copper engraving of the Emperor's triumphal procession by Albrecht Dürer, the most unobtrusive clerk could buy his picture of the world on the way home or on the way to work folded in his coat pocket and by that very act demonstrate his mastery over his environment. The picture of the world provided by the Harmsworth Press was more glamorous than anything that the denominational papers or even *Y Faner* could manage; and when David Lloyd George got going he needed a team of Dürers to portray his performance as one of the four horsemen of the Apocalypse.

In the same year that the Daily Mail was born, August and Louis Lumiere opened their first cinema in Paris. From this time forward the common man's picture of the world was liable to movement as if an invisible poltergeist were constantly shifting the furniture of his imagination. In less than a generation D. W. Griffiths, who liked to claim descent from 'Griffith King of Wales', had created the film language which was to ensure that the moving picture would finally displace the printed word as the universal means of satisfying the appetite for fiction. Whereas the Welsh had been able to cope very well with the technology of the printing press, the new media arrived at their doorstep at a time of outward turmoil and inner confusion. Nothing illustrates this more clearly than the history of the Rhondda valleys. In 1902 a new Education Act, with the inevitable help of Lloyd George, saw to it that Wales was given a pattern of secondary education which took a new generation further down the road that led them away from their indigenous culture. In 1904 the Rhondda, like the rest of Wales, was boiling over in the heat of a religious revival with a population reaching up frantically for those ropes of salvation which are also the last links with the old Welsh way of life, the old language and the sense of security, self-respect and self confidence that went with it. In less than ten years the heat of the revival was transformed into an equally ardent enthusiasm in favour of the war against Germany and an unrestrained pride in the new brand of jingoistic imperialism provided for them by the powerful combination of the London press and Mr. Lloyd George. In less than ten years after that in the midst of economic suffering, this warm hearted community embraced socialism, caught between the calculating caution of the official Labour party and an impulsive desire to support the idealism of young Marxist leaders.

xi

The one thing the Welsh did not have in order to face the New Media and all the challenges it presented was confidence in themselves and in the intrinsic value of their own culture. There are of course many factors which can contribute to the undermining of the will to persist in the face of social changes of seismographic proportions. (This is almost a discipline in itself and it has become a central study for anyone interested in the European condition.) When the melting pot has so much to offer, why not just jump in? If the security and material welfare of Western Europe depend so heavily on the American nuclear arsenal, why do we not all follow the example of so many of our 19th century relations and apply directly to Congress for admission as additional states? In this respect it does no harm for us to take a look at what has happened and what is happening to the culture of the remnants of Indian nations in North America. Much work has been done among the Hopi, the Suni, the Pawnee and particularly the Navaho. By some accounts there appear to be tribes among the Navaho who cherish a song or a ritual to heal every ailment, to meet most emergencies and to welcome every day. To these nations language is in fact both a fortress and a fold in which are preserved the hundreds of rituals and songs essential to their existence; even more essential to their wellbeing, in their view, than their flocks and herds. It is because of the importance that they attach to this system of speech and the way in which it enshrines the meaning of their existence that they are unwilling to attend the schools provided for them by the Federal Government because English is the medium of instruction. They have come to regard their language as the last line of defence to keep out the elements of an alien industrial culture which threatens a way of life which they believe to be tied in through their culture and language to the true meaning of existence.

Far be it from me to equate the industrious and ambitious Welsh with a bunch of unprogressive Indians. Nevertheless we are obliged to record that in the Welsh Reservations the education system after 1870 was exclusively in English. The tribal Sunday Schools continued to be solely responsible for literacy in Welsh. For most people this seemed a satisfactory arrangement. When the chapels were full in a place like Merthyr Tydfil where the population was still overwhelmingly Welsh speaking there were eight Sunday School teachers to every one professional beavering away in the State Schools. But the foundations of the old way of life were already giving way. Loss of religious certainties was of course in no way peculiar to Wales. What the Welsh lost in addition was confidence in their own identity. The badge of all the tribes and the basis of any teneable claim to separate nationality had always been the language. Now all the forces of change, spearheaded by a comprehensive education system from the infant school to the university seemed to be telling them that their language and for that matter their

131

antiquated religion were no better than chains around their feet. When a character called Ann Evans, in Kate Roberts's brilliant novel 'Traed Mewn Cyffion' whispers in her neighbours' ear at a school prize day 'Da y gŵyr Duw i bwy i ro B.A.'. (Well doth God know to whom to give the B.A.) she is not only making a quiet joke at the expense of the row of teachers in their black mortar boards and gowns. She is making a tacit acknowledgement that both providence and progress are on the side of this mighty language which she herself cannot speak.

As a sop to the remnants of their national pride, the leaders of Welsh life made greater use of the word 'national' to designate their public institutions at the very time when the genuine ties of nationality were weakening and falling away. The national university for example managed to attract support from colliers and quarrymen with vague though passionate appeal to national sentiment. They even talked of Owen Glyndwr, but their real inspiration was Owen's College Manchester, and it was in those echoing green brick corridors that so many of the brightest children of the 'werin' first learnt to despise so many of the characteristics cherished by their parents and grandparents. Instead of celebrating the national being, in the manner common to all national universities from Oslo to Jerusalem and Washington to Warsaw, the University of Wales flourished on the basis of whatever provincial contribution it could make to English imperial power. A political or economic historian might argue that in this respect the University was doing no more than reflecting accurately the realities of power. This might well be so, but it cannot be allowed to camouflage the damage done to the Welsh psyche. A conspicuous feature of the Welsh condition in the twentieth century has been that sociological phenomenon known as 'culture shame'. It is almost part of the condition that it should be so little studied. Like a secret vice or an incurable disease, it is rarely mentioned. But from time to time it breaks out in unexpected eruptions of 'culture hatred' most frequently directed against the Welsh language. What used to be an atavistic Anglo-Saxon racial hatred for the unintelligible lingo of a welshing Taffy now manifests itself in a Welsh County Councillor's abrupt irrational outburst against 'any more of this Welsh business'.

xii

It will be seen that both radio and cinema arrived in Wales at a singularly inauspicious time. There were no effective channels open for them to make any contribution to bolstering up the native culture or injecting it with exciting new life. There was a direct link between the absence of technical capability and the nature of existing scholarship and educational facilities. Well before the first World War the philosophic base of the social application of science had hardened. Practical capitalists and theoretic socialists were united in their passionate devotion to the concept of scientific necessity: and in popular terms this filtered through to the common consciousness in the form of a vague but potent religion of progress. History was transformed into a machine driven by this new god. What little chance human beings had of influencing the direction the vehicle might take was no more than the degree of trust it was prepared to invest in the god's goodwill. This was not difficult for a theo-retically Calvinist people. But the new version proved to be far less creative than the original. Instead of stimulating, it deadened response. The presence of the god of the machine was so evident, so omnipotent and so lacking in mystery that the only effective worship appeared to be a condition of helplessness that amounted to little better than spiritual slavery. Machinery was the church militant on earth and the machinery of govern-ment was only one of its less noisy but more sinister manifesta-tions. The only way to really please this god was to demonstrate complete submission by lining up into endless rows of uniform units for the sacred purpose of listening to the perfection of a self existent heart beat. In this new church little Welsh children were never asked to recite verses in public, or to take part in chapel meetings or even contribute to the ministry or the mis-sionary fund. Their only duty was to remain helpless and silent, and among well-brought-up children what could have been easier than that?

xiii

Radio came to Wales in the shape of the B.B.C., as an exten-sion of that middle-class English culture which we described earlier as radiating from its vantage point so close to the heart of the Empire. Cardiff functioned as a colonial sub-post office to

133

Bristol and it took many years of campaigning before anything that could be described as a Welsh region was established. The first big struggle was to get any Welsh speaking Welshmen established on the staff; and the second was to separate Wales from the West of England and give it some semblance of being a national service. All this took many years to achieve and might never have been achieved but for unlikely collaboration between two of the most talented and probably most untypical Welshmen around at that crucial time. But for a period of wholehearted collaboration between the aging Lloyd George and the still young Saunders Lewis it is very unlikely that the Weksh region would ever have been established. Presumably the minutes of those stormy meetings with the Director General of the B.B.C. must still lie in the archives of the University Registry. Had the Welsh committee not been led by an ex-Prime Minister, Sir John Reith, with his Messianic vision of English culture circulating the globe, would never have given way. And in any case it has to be admitted that the service provided was sketchy and the whole operation remained firmly under central control from London.

There was in fact a curious parallel between the position of the Welsh staff of the B.B.C. and those refugees from the film industry taking refuge in Alexandra Palace in the immediate post war period. The war had brought no benefit to Welsh broadcasting. Anything to do with Welsh culture was a luxury to be sacrificed along with bananas, silk stockings and soft centred chocolates. Film had had a much more important role to play. It was only afterwards that the documentary appeared to become as expendable as Welsh and was roughly discarded in the last dash for imperial glory on celluloid.

Inside the B.B.C. the former documentary film makers found themselves unhappy prisoners of an uncongenial atmosphere. In the first place television was no more than an extension of the broadcasting signal into a sufficient size to accommodate a picture as well as sound. The primitive television studio was no more than a garishly lit expansion of the old sound studio. In a curious echo of what happened in the film industry, the microphone remained firmly on its throne at the centre of the operation, while cumbersome cameras bowed in obeisance from all sides. Along with the microphone went the accent, the impeccable tones of men like Stuart Hibberd, John Snagge and Alvar Liddel. The B.B.C. remained the custodian of English oral culture and this in turn reflected the grim determination of the English middle class to hang on to its essentially aristocratic heritage. Like English Literature that accent was the product of four and a half centuries material power, the crowning glory which gave them the right to an outstanding position among the nations of the earth. The microphone like the accent was safe in the hands of cultural civil servants, a lay clergy robed to dispense the sacraments and national treasures; custodians and conservers. In contrast, the men from the documentary film world saw themselves as artists. They knew that there was a living relationship between the nature of their medium and a revolutionary approach to the world. Their subject was the life of the masses and the world was their parish. They were the legitimate heirs of the first art form to emerge directly from an industrial civilisation. They knew that history was on their side and yet the condition of their employment and the comforts that went with their status depend on their loyalty to a benevolent Corporation which had given them shelter.

During the period of their fretful inactivity in Alexandra Palace, the situation in Wales had taken a turn for the better. Substations were opened in the North and the West. Men and women of exceptional talent were recruited to produce programmes in English and Welsh and for a period of ten years or more it could be claimed that B.B.C. Radio played an active and constructive part in Welsh cultural life, possibly the leading part at a time when very little creative activity could be discerned in other directions. The output did its best to cover the full spectrum of cultural activity from children's programmes and comedy shows features and drama to the sophisticated poetry of Kitchener Davies, David Jones, Dylan Thomas and Robert Williams Parry. There could hardly have been a time when Welshness in both languages benefited more from the impact of the new medium of radio technology. Once again, as in the story of the brief heyday of the silent cinema, it could not last. It was not merely a case of the Welsh producers inside the super-structure of a London cultural civil service. (Their time and effort and capabilities were always strictly limited to what they could insert into the vacant slots of an omni-present and omnipotent London Home Service.) The time-bomb of technical development was ticking away. Television was growing up and getting too big for the confines of Alexandra Palace. In the words of the old Welsh proverb, the year old frog was now ready to swallow its parent.

A new Television Centre was opened at Lime Grove. (This explains why for many years the majority of television technicians spoke with a Shepherd's Bush accent.) The experience of America had already demonstrated that television was the medium of the future, capable of swallowing both radio and film. Inevitably there were power struggles. The headquarters in the battleship at Portland Place kept a firm hold on the purse strings. It also attempted to control the content and style of television programmes. One of the refugees from documentary film Andrew Miller-Jones succeeded with the help of a lively journalist called Malcolm Muggeridge to establish a programme that was in the Grierson tradition of a window on the world. It was called Panorama and it has survived to this day, almost as a living memorial of a compromise that was achieved between the middle class ethos of the B.B.C. and the freewheeling interest in the human spectacle of the old documentary movement. This compromise could have lasted indefinitely but for a surge of interest in the City of London. By the mid 1950's capitalists had become keenly aware of the potential of television for the exercise of the gentle art of printing money.

The advent of commercial television in 1956 dealt the death blow to the supremacy of the microphone and the concept of cultural civil service which had governed the B.B.C. from its inception. 1956 was a watershed year and it is still difficult to disentangle cause and effect among the upheavals of that period. Anthony Eden and a concept of Empire went down the drain at Suez. The cosy notion of a friendly Russian bear met its end on the streets of Budapest. In the London theatre the French windows of Terrence Rattigan were blown out by the young men intent on looking back in anger ready to reproach everybody and everything for their own inadequacies and sense of deprivation. But by far the most far-reaching change was brought about by commercial television. This capitalist's cash register turned out to be Leon Trotsky's secret weapon. It provided the answer to the Marxist dilemma concerning how much bourgeois culture should continue to be nurtured after the revolution and how much proletarian art would be needed to replace the decadent outmoded culture of the centuries of oppression. Commercial television discovered two things which had been largely overlooked by a B.B.C. mesmerised by elegance and refinement: the working class and the North of England. This coincided happily with a fresh surge of creativity among the people of England. Typically a new school of dramatists and actors were given their chance. (Osborne, Wesker, Storey, Arden, Pinter, O'Toole, Finney, etc.) It seemed as if with characteristic stoicism, the English would waste no time or tears lamenting the passing of their Empire before gathering themselves together and preparing for a fresh onslaught to create another one in the new medium offering itself for exploitation. Here at least in a world of dwindling markets they would create a growth industry which they could look on with pride and call the best in the world.

xiv

Needless to say the people of Wales, Welsh or English speaking, were not given the opportunity for a parallel revival. When television arrived like Hengist and Horsa it brought with it the Treachery of the Long Masts. Wenvoe and St. Hilary were sites outside Cardiff facing the Bristol Channel. The masts were there not in the service of Wales but in the service of the religion of the self-existent machine, the god of progress, whose mysterious ways had never been ours to question. Well-brought-up sons of the Manse could declare that they were speaking as servants of the B.B.C. or I.T.V. and not as Welshmen, and this declaration of the purity of their intent could be widely accepted as the hallmark of integrity and dedication. It seemed as if the education system had removed any trace of self-respect along with their self-confidence. It was no longer part of the Welsh character to reason why; only to accept change in the cheerful spirit of a drugged patient on his way to a cultural operating theatre where his individuality would be removed by a painless operation roughly parallel with a frontal lobotomy.

The development of television over the last quarter of a century has been dominated by the extraordinary form of competition between the B.B.C. and Commercial Television which

137

Professor Tom Burns in his study of the B.B.C. *'Public Institution and Private World'* has described as 'pacing'. When two runners keep up with each other on an otherwise empty track, what they are engaged on is not a race. It is a perpetual training session conducted in a private world to ensure that both runners are fit enough to defeat any other competitor that might wish to join in a race. In this private world the battles which go on are not those that the public imagines it is witnessing. Dog does not eat dog. All their actions even when they appear to be in conflict are in fact mutually supportive. If for example the B.B.C. succeeds in buying a new hair-raising series from the United States, it becomes absolutely essential that the I.T.V. companies do exactly the same as quickly as possible. And if a B.B.C. expert produces impressive findings to prove that there is no relationship whatsoever between violence in television programmes and vandalism among the young, it is always necessary for an authority from the 'independent' side to pop up with his own array of statistics to confirm his learned colleague's findings. On either side, producers and administrators have much more in common with each other than with the public they profess to serve and for whose affections they pretend to compete. The higher up the ladder of command, the easier it is for the dedicated 'professional' to change sides. They are media men living in a media orientated world and by now operating more closely to the seat of power than was ever the lot of Sir John Reith. He never became Viceroy of India and he never achieved the kind of intimacy with Prime Ministers and members of Cabinet that he would have liked. His faceless successors enjoy far more power. They are in fact Viceroys of an electronic empire and the institutions they control have become the most influential in British life. With the passage of time their positions have become more entrenched and any change attempted in the order of fixed and immutable television becomes tantamount to a constitutional change of revolutionary proportions.

During this same period, the story of the New Media in Wales and its impact on Welshness and Welsh culture has not been encouraging. There has been an alarming decline in the percentage of Welsh speakers among the population and television may well have accelerated this process. This is a difficult calculation to make and significant figures are not easy to come by. But no one can deny a general sense of unease. The television set has insinuated itself like a sinister visitor from an alien universe and sits in the corner of every household exerting its hypnotic rays and quietly changing the natures of the inmates even as they go about their daily business. Its greatest influence is assumed to be over the children. It has a hold over their imaginations and their thought processes which make the influence of mediaeval story-tellers and Jesuit priests pale into insignificance. That phosphorescent glow, those luminous and beguiling colours, sap the will and undermine the individuality of people, transforming them into worshippers of this latest soporific extension of that self existent heart-beat, that universal religion that demands nothing more from its adherents than total passivity. All this may sound like a gross exaggeration, and yet our Welsh experience tells us that it must contain more than the grain of truth. This is the new opium of the people that will carry them over from the eternal arms of one religion into the grasp of another; that will tide them across the discomforts and disturbances of the unhappy process of 'culture shift'. It will be television that will transform all those (shifty, shifting, unsure,) hypocritical, welshing, deceitful, untrustworthy, disloyal, unintelligible Taffs into firm cuddly gonks manufactured in the shapes suggested by those popular entertainers who manage to stumble on one way or another of making some sort of Welshness acceptable to the great British-that-is-English public. Again this is an exaggeration, but the truly alarming thought is that such a process would not meet with the disapproval of the satraps of the medium and that they would more than likely go out of their way to encourage it, even demand it, if it improved their ratings, or gained them signs of approval from their invisible masters.

An attempt was made in the early sixties to create something like an independent television service for North and West Wales. It came too late to the feast, and what crumbs it could pick up from the floor were not enough to keep it alive. It was run by starry-eyed educationalists, ministers and trade-unionists without sufficient experience or capital. By the 'professionals' in the B.B.C. and I.T.V. their failure was greeted with chuckles of secret delight. It seemed to confirm once and for all that television had no place for amateurs however enthusiastic or well-intentioned. It was a closed shop to be quietly divided up between management, producing staff, and unions. This was to be the standard working arrangement: a sandwich with a thin spread of programme output in the middle. No sooner was something called B.B.C. Wales established than B.B.C.Two. emerged to demand a lion's share of B.B.C. finances on the grounds that it was going to provide a better class of programmes for a better class of people. The old spirit of Portland Place and English middle class culture was reasserting itself and regrouping within the confines of the new television empire. Driven on by the process of 'pacing' both the B.B.C. and I.T.V. plunged on into the realm of colour television. This trebled their expenses at a stroke and the development of such a thing as B.B.C. Wales came very low down in the order of priority. A characteristic of the sixties and the seventies was the intensification of the struggle between workers and management for their share of the production cake in a Labour controlled mixed economy. This struggle was very accurately reflected in the private world of television. While the pacing went on, the real conflicts were between rival unions and between management and union members. Discontent was particularly rife in the B.B.C. whose financial resources were more restricted. The net result on both channels was less finance for programmes and more for profits and wages. In Wales again promised developments were postponed and the quality of programmes often suffered through inadequate finances.

It is perfectly obvious even to the most casual and unconcerned observer that neither the B.B.C. nor the reigning I.T.V. company have any primary concern or committment to anything that could be described as Welsh culture. The B.B.C. quite rightly claims pride of place among those institutions which exist to defend and propagate the English heritage. In this respect it does more than Parliament or the Press, than the Universities or the established Church, than the Arts Council and all the celebrated institutions to which this important body gives its financial and moral support. What it has done for Wales has always been minimal and incidental. However anxious it showed itself in the post war period to recruit a conspicuous number of Welsh speaking men and women on its producing staff, the total operation was always geared to the requirements of London. There might be well-known Welsh faces in the window of the front office, so to speak, but the factory itself was a branch-office fully integrated into the main operation and turning out useful spare parts. Producing staff understood perfectly well that what they did for local consumption was no more than gentle exercise on the nursery slope. The proper ambition and career module was to think of something acceptable for Head Office and suitable contributions for the network. This species of work ethic automatically relegated the Welsh language to the status of a second class citizen even among professionals who had been recruited on the basis of their creative abilities in that language. The complexity of the situation was compounded by the demands of the non-Welsh-speaking staff for status and budgets commensurate with the increasing percentage of non Welsh speakers inside the 'Welsh region'. In the spirit of the B.B.C. charter they were able to argue their obligation to maintain a service that would inform, educate and entertain this ever increasing majority of the Welsh people. And with every year that passed under this system it was more than likely that the majority would grow rapidly. There was nothing in the B.B.C. charter about defending or propagating the Welsh heritage.

In the late sixties T.W.W. lost its franchise as the company responsible for Independent Television in Wales and the West of England. Part of the reason given for their dismissal was the inadequate provision and unsatisfactory material they had produced in the Welsh language and in Wales generally. A galaxy of showbusiness talent and Welsh language establishment figures made common cause with somewhat more hard-headed Bristol-based businessmen to create H.T.V. They were lavish with their promises to usher in a new era of creative television which would make an unprecedented impact on Welsh life and generally invigorate cultural life in Wales. They did what they could. Their track record was certainly an improvement on their predecessor. They made notable contributions to children's programmes, to Welsh news, to opera, to the less expensive type of discussion programme, to strictly literary matters, to the Eisteddfod and they made a start with independent drama in both languages. Whatever their intentions there was

141

no way in which they could overcome the growing rigidity of the structure of television in the United Kingdom as a whole. In London the controlling powers of the two giant organizations sat side by side like Gog and Magog each with a leg raised ready to go out pacing the moment any impatient enquirer should stop to ask them exactly what they were doing. The B.B.C. was welding the entire United Kingdom into one big suburban happy-family, and the I.T.V. was doing the same along with the commendable activity of making healthy profits.

When these basic Anglo-Saxon attitudes were transferred to the situation in Wales, it soon became obvious that they were painfully irrelevant to our problem: indeed they actively exacerbated it. Television pacing in Wales meant a peculiarly wasteful exercise in which the further-flung servants of Gog and Magog engaged themselves busily in mirror-image making, duplicating each other's programmes with comic persistence whenever the tight London schedules allowed them to pop their heads nervously out of the ubiquitous box. The principle of television pacing ruled out what was one of the most immediately obvious solutions to Welsh problems, namely constructive co-operation between B.B.C. Wales and H.T.V. Wales. When the possibilities of bringing to bear dual resources in collaborative efforts or even co-productions were suggested in the early seventies,—at a time when the B.B.C. had begun to collaborate with Time-Life and with Communist television organisations beyond the iron curtain,—it was pointed out by those in authority and control that a public service corporation like the B.B.C. could never be expected to soil its hands in enterprises that would also involve too close contact with the sullied servants of commerce. It took ten years of strenuous sacrifice, chiefly on the part of Cymdeithas yr Iaith Gymraeg, to make any noticeable impression on the complacent surface of this attitude.

xv

It is at this point that we may once more observe the curious and telling coincidence of interest between those restless heirs of the creative documentary film tradition, comfortably trapped inside the metropolitan television structures, and the defenders of the Welsh language under siege, and those producers in Wales most concerned with turning the power of the new media around and directing it towards the supporting, sustaining and enlarging of the indigenous culture, instead of wiping it out. It is an aspect worth dwelling on if only because it is a heartening feature of what otherwise would be a very sad history indeed. This coincidence of interest in itself suggests that human creativity, at all times and in all places, and even in the impersonal mechanised world of television, is one and indivisible. And more than that, that an element of genuine freedom is an indispensable ingredient of the creative process.

An early day motion for a debate on the nature of the Fourth Channel was tabled in the House of Commons on December 2nd, 1971. Before this a group of television and film directors and critics had organised themselves into a campaign to stop the five largest commercial companies from getting their greedy hands on the Fourth Channel. The basis of their protest was a rejection of both existing broadcasting systems. They saw the Fourth Channel as a natural forum for a freer and more enlightened use of the television medium, available to all the people, to independent creative programme-makers and not tied to the monolithic tyranny of either the B.B.C. or the I.T.V. This was the origin of the movement that ultimately found rational expression in the celebrated Annan Report. By now it looks pretty certain that the Fourth Channel when it eventually appears will be a characteristically pragmatic English compromise based on the philosophy and some of the ideals laid down by the campaign of the creative producers that began in 1971.

In Wales campaigns for cultural values had begun much earlier and on a much wider front, and as usual had proved far more costly, and had gained far less. Cymdeithas Yr Iaith Gymraeg (The Welsh Language Society) had come into existence in 1962 mainly as a youthful response to Saunders Lewis's sombre B.B.C. annual radio lecture, Tynged Yr Iaith (The Fate of the Language). As if some inexorable wheel had turned full circle, the most acute critical mind at work in the Welsh language was concentrating our attention on the crisis point in the condition of our culture. As far as the new media were concerned, the control of television now played the role that the control of radio had occupied in the struggles of the early 1930's. But this time the defenders of the language were on much weaker ground. An economic depression, another world war, the triumph of a British Labour Party, popular broadcasting, alien education, a mass retreat from nonconformity and organised religion, had left the Welsh language and the Welsh identity in what appeared to be an indefensible position. There was no ex-Prime Minister around to champion the cause in the corridors of power. Some senior Labour politicians were still capable of making their sentimental sentiments known once a year on the National Eisteddfod platform. But in spite of the power and the positions they held, or perhaps because of them, they showed as many signs of active concern and practical determination as a row of sleeping beauties in an opium den. It was as if the corpse of Welsh culture had been measured and that all that remained was to make the necessary funeral arrangements. It says much for Mr. Lewis's influence that one rare broadcast in his unmistakable voice was sufficient to activate the brightest spirits of the new generation that were still able to understand the language in which he spoke. Like Emrys Wledig in the celebrated speech of his 1936 verse play *Buchedd Garmon*, also written for radio, the broadcast summoned the Welsh people to the defence of their heritage.

The prolonged contemplation of history, ancient or modern, is never without its warnings or its consolations. Even the remote past can sometimes appear astonishingly relevant. From the very origin of the Welsh as a distinct nation, it is possible to discern two contrasting standards of behaviour, often in conflict, sometimes co-existing uncomfortably in the career of some striking personality. Over the centuries they appear to have made themselves indispensable both to the Welsh character and to the vitality of the Welsh tradition. The more successful and aggressive model was rooted in the agreeable fantasy that the whole of the island had once belonged to the Cambro-British (i.e. the Welsh) ruling class. Like fantasies it satisfied a frustrated appetite. Generation after generation it encouraged the warrior aristocracy in the painful day to day business of defending a Wales and a Welshness that in historic perspective appears to have been under constant attack. Their task was bloody, onerous and painful, but their mythology promised them rich rewards in this world and the next.

Another attitude had a totally religious origin and purpose.

Dewi Sant like all the other Celtic saints belonged to exactly the same network of aristocratic families as the ambitious warriors: but the solution he offered to the pressing problems of maintaining the integrity of a precarious Welsh civilisation were very different. His appeal was to asceticism and altruism. He called upon the people to make sacrifices for the good of their souls and not for any material advantage or for the pursuit of the will-o-the-wisp of neo-imperial glory on the strength of their vaunted Romano-British inheritance. If we were to apply this interpretation of the Welsh tradition to any period in our past it would at least have the merit of relating the marmoreal shapes of academic history to the continuing problem of human behaviour. The long history of a small nation is a convenient receptacle for growing a culture that may enable us to diagnose with greater accuracy notable ailments of the human condition. It is possible to argue that without a stubborn strain of altruism the Welsh people would never have remained loyal to their language through all the storms and stresses of the last four and a half centuries. At any point in time, from the Tudor triumph at the Battle of Bosworth, which the bards hailed as the consummation of all the ancient prophesies about reconquering the Isle of Britain, there were always powerful and influential Welshmen busily ennumerating the material benefits that would flow directly from casting off the shackles of the ancient language. Again it could be argued that it was the ascetic and altruistic strain that was responsible for the more creative aspects of Welsh Dissent in the eighteenth century. The remarkable movements among the peasantry and working class in the nineteenth century would never have been possible without the exercise of this most attractive aspect of the Welsh character.

In this perspective, it becomes wholly appropriate that the present day activists should be conscious of their own descent from this tradition; the children of Dissent in Wales have become responsible for the creation of the first authentic dissident movement in Britain. If one wished to single out the most creative contribution that the advent of television has made to Welsh life, the simple answer would have to be Cymdeithas yr Iaith. Without counting the cost, and in an unbroken sequence of imprisonments and fines, this society of young people has been prepared to challenge the might of the modern state in order to seek justice for this same language that has survived the centuries, in order to give it the opportunity to live and thrive in the modern world.

No doubt the cause was that much more attractive to the young because it was so opposed to the gross materialism and economic determinism of the age. The generosity of youth will always find an appropriate outlet. But I think it is as well for every Welshman now to realise whether he lives in Abergavenny or Aberystwyth, or even in Liverpool or London, that he owes a special debt to these young people. With their own lives as their only resource they have made themselves the custodians of a very battered Ark of the Covenant. They remind us that the land and the language of Wales are the natural repositories of the memorials of two thousand years of Welsh existence. They contain the shrines of history, the evidence of a people's struggle to preserve the right to live in their own way; what would now be called the fight for freedom and self-determination. In the tradition of the dissidents and of Dewi Sant their protests are rooted in non-violent civil disobedience; and the health of our society and of our civilisation may well be measured by our response to their challenge.

Certainly no creative artist, whatever medium he works in can ignore it. If he does, the work he produces is likely to be immeasurably reduced in stature and significance. What they are telling us is not new. They are saying that our history is worthy of respect and so is our land and so is our language. These are living elements that have always existed for our wellbeing. We would be less than worthy if we failed them and used indifference to betray the spirit they represent.

Here, as in any other corner of the globe, television is the visual agent of the potential for destruction that must exist in the superstructure of a selfexistent Machine that increasingly strives towards a perfection of serving itself and its own purposes, irrespective of any society that makes use of it. History has already shown that the forces of technology can only be kept in check and made to serve creative and socially beneficient ends by societies that still have the will to continue to celebrate their own existence. Welsh culture, the ancient land and language at its core, has as much right as any other to expect the new media to participate fully in this creative task.